GRIZZLY LOVER

C.D. GORRI

Grizzly Lover

Purely Paranormal Pleasures
by C.D. Gorri
Edited by T.P. BookNookNuts
Formatted by Amanda Kimberley MysticWorldsInkPublicationsandDesign
Copyright 2020 C.D. Gorri

To all of you who leave reviews, thank you so much for telling others about your experience with reading my books. It is very much appreciated. Xoxo,
C.D.

HELLO READERS!

Thank you for purchasing this Purely Paranormal Pleasures tale! Can a bad-tempered Bear learn to forgive? I hope you enjoy Teresa's and Oliver's tale.

Purely Paranormal Pleasures will transport you into the realm of sensuous, spellbinding Alphas and their captivating mates. There are no rules…. Only pure pleasure.

These tales are delivered up by 3 master MAVENS of paranormal P. Mattern, C.D. Gorri, and Amanda Kimberley.

Happy reading!
Xoxo,
C.D. Gorri

TAGLINE:

Teresa broke Oliver's heart once before, but now she needs his help. Can her Grizzly lover put the past behind them?

Oliver Pax is one of the most prolific composers of all time. He is the award-winning writer of such Broadway hits as The Beast of Brooklyn Heights and its upcoming conclusion Where Beauty Lives. A loner known for his grumpy and secretive nature, the reclusive Grizzly Bear Shifter is in for the shock of his life when a blast from his past washes up on his doorstep after a terrible accident.

Teresa Witherspoon has been on the run for the past two years. She's traveled across the country and back again fearing the day her father and his henchmen find her and her son. Caring for Thomas has kept her going this far, but when an accident leaves her hospitalized, she has no choice but to call the one person she swore to stay away from.

Will the Grizzly Bear Shifter she'd once loved help her in her time of need?

"Resa," Oliver fisted the note he'd found tucked under the secondhand keyboard he'd just finished paying off.

The instrument sat against one wall of the cramped room, right beside the only window in the small Brooklyn Heights apartment he'd been renting the past six months since he came to the city.

For a Grizzly Bear Shifter used to the wilds of the woods as his backyard, it was quite the change, but he just had to try to see if he could make a go of his music. Oliver had always been gifted with a good ear, but even as a cub, his mother had encouraged him to go and seek his destiny.

Brooklyn Heights was as close to Manhattan as he could afford with his meager savings, but what did money matter anyway? Especially when there was music to be written. The window faced the south brick wall of another small apartment complex identical to his.

It didn't matter what it looked like outside, as long as he was able to breathe some fresh air. At least on the fifth floor, it was somewhat fresher than the heavily congested streets below.

She was gone. His mind registered that fact as he took in the empty room. She'd left.

"No," he growled, and aimed his fist at the tiled counter top, cracking a few of the old ceramic squares in the process. Mrs. Goldstein, the landlady, would be pissed when she saw that.

Oliver's Bear roared inside of him and his heart contracted painfully in his chest. It was worse than being sucker punched by Thor his idiot cousin, who was as big and strong as his namesake. Why would Teresa say such cruel things? He couldn't believe it, couldn't fathom his sweet Resa saying such foul callous words about their relationship. He read the hated missive one more time.

Oliver,

It was fun while it lasted, but even you can't be so naïve as to think I could find true love with a nobody. I just wanted to get back at my father. Don't bother looking for me or calling, I will have already changed my number.

Teresa

Yes, it was her handwriting. He closed his eyes on the wave of anguish that washed over him. Gasping, he sunk to his knees while the beast inside of him roared and stomped his massive claws in fury.

Mate, his Bear cried out, but Oliver refused to answer his other half.

How could she just leave him like this? He'd been so sure of her, of them. He was positive that she loved him too. Being with her was everything to him. She was his fated mate. It was the first time he had ever tasted happiness. A taste that was bitter now that he knew it was all one-sided.

The first time he'd seen the golden-haired beauty, Oliver's Grizzly Bear had stood up and taken notice. The second he'd breathed in her peaches and cream scent, his animal had roared one single word in his mind's eye that would change Oliver's life forever.

Mate.

Following his heart, he'd approached the soft spoken, elegantly dressed Teresa Witherspoon after spying her at the park day after day. She'd sit on one of the cleaner benches and read from a book of seventeenth century cavalier poets.

"You like Lovelace? Looking at you I pictured a Donne fan," Oliver said when he'd finally found the nerve to *approach her.*

"Spiritualist poetry doesn't appeal as much to me I guess. I like Lovelace and Suckling. They're fun and witty."

"But they're just trying to get in a girl's pants with their poetry. You approve?" he grinned.

"It's not so much the seduction that appeals to me, it's the living in the moment. Carpe diem and all that," she *shrugged.*

There was something so tragically sad about her that his heart had squeezed in his chest with longing. He'd wanted to make her smile. Heck, he even pretended to stumble in the grass, laid himself flat just to get her to walk over and touch him. And she had, put her soft, long hands right on him to see if he was alright. He'd stolen a kiss and had never looked back. Until now. The dream was over. She'd left him.

Oliver's Bear roared in his grief. That last night they were together, he'd told her the truth about what he was. The fact that there were more things in the world than she had ever imagined.

Oliver Pax had committed a most grievous sin against

his Clan. He'd confessed to a normal, a human woman, that he was a Grizzly Bear Shifter.

It was allowed under certain circumstances, like when the woman in question was your fated mate. He'd thought she'd taken it well, after all, they'd made wild, passionate love immediately after. Hell, he'd been so caught up in the moment, he'd marked her with his bite, tying himself to her irrevocably, but now she was gone.

What would become of him? Would he go mad like so many other Shifters who'd lost their mates? He had heard the stories. The tales of broken matings and rogue Shifters who needed to be put down.

Oliver tipped the bottle of whiskey back emptying its fiery contents down his throat. Then he threw the hated thing across the room. Something about the muted violence of the act satisfied his animal's need for savagery. The Bear inside of him wanted to tear the whole world down, but maybe work would be a better outlet, he thought.

Oliver sat down at his banged up keyboard and began to play. He poured out his bruised heart. Wrote lyrics and tied them together with a fairy tale as old as they come. The Beast of Brooklyn Heights was born that day. And the rest, as they say, was history.

CHAPTER ONE

A *couple of years later…*

Cameras flashed as reporters shoved their equipment in his face despite the pouring rain. Oliver Pax did his best to get through them as he attempted to leave the *Madoc Grand Theatre*. The beast in him wanted to snarl and snap his teeth, but these were *normals* and he had to keep the secret of the supernatural world.

It was his duty, and he'd already transgressed on that once before. No, he pushed the thought of her out of his mind. She would not haunt him here. Not tonight.

The buzzards seemed immune to the thunderstorm that was brewing around them, but not Oliver. The scent of ozone had the hair on the back of his neck standing straight up. It was bound to be a nasty one.

He blinked under the bright marquee and grinned despite himself. Chance Madoc had bought and refurbished the old rundown eyesore of a theatre and had turned it into something grand and useful. It was, Oliver had to admit, an amazing old place. The acoustics were simply sublime.

Of course, he'd come straight to Oliver asking him to allow the "golden boy of Broadway" first dibs on producing his latest at the new site. *Surviving On Breadcrumbs*, was a smash hit.

Oliver's newest musical was a retelling of the classic fairytale featuring Hansel and Gretel. In this version, the infamous twins were actually a pair of bounty hunters looking for witches and supernatural creatures in order to hunt them down and kill them. The pair meets out death and violence wherever they go, until Gretel falls in love with a Werewolf, and has a consequential change of heart.

It was a silly thing really, a secret hidden wish of his own, but Oliver would never reveal something so personal. So, he covered it up, with dark humor, and an appropriate amount of blood and gore. Add to it a fantastic musical score that he was told would translate well to film, and bam, a hit was born.

Or so his agent had said once the deal from Hollywood came in just that morning to the little man's unending delight. Whatever. Money, fame, they did not matter. His work was an outlet for his pain and sorrow. Feelings that could lead to much worse if his Bear ever tipped the scales from barely hanging on to his sanity to going rogue.

Oliver worked night and day to make sure that never happened. It was the only way to appease the beast, and to keep his fragile hold on his stability. Thunder cracked and a flash of lightning brightened the crowded walkway that led to the theatre doors. He ignored the gasp of the crowd and stood still like a deer in headlights. For one solitary moment, Oliver thought he'd seen a ghost.

"Smile Pax, you've got another hit on your hand," Chance Madoc slapped him on the back jovially, jogging him from his fancy.

Good thing too, he supposed. Visions like that were dangerous to his health, and to others. Chance nodded at the paparazzi who were trying desperately to get Oliver's attention at that very same moment.

"You know I hate this circus," he snarled at the half-Demon who was also one of his closest friends.

Not that he had very many of those to boast about. Still, Chance was a fair man. He believed in Oliver when he was new and unknown. Hell, he'd given him a leg up and Oliver never forgot it. A couple of years might be a flash in the pan to most Shifters, but it was a long time in the fickle eyes of fame.

"Why aren't you waiting for your wife?" Oliver asked the man curtly.

Leandra Katrell-Madoc was Chance's mate and wife, not to mention the star of Oliver's first mega hit, *The Beast of Brooklyn Heights*. She was a lovely woman, a supremely talented songstress, and besides that, Oliver liked her. She was spunky and more than fair.

She didn't complain the way most stars did about his notes or direction. Even when he'd asked her to play the Witch in this new show, as opposed to the younger starring role of Gretel. Yes, he liked her. Leandra had integrity. Something far too many people lacked in his not-so-humble opinion.

"She'll be along in a moment. So, where are you with, *Where Beauty Lives?* The pages are late, Pax, that's not like you."

Oliver had been waiting for the question. Chance had been patient, but the half-Demon never failed to mention the fact that Oliver was late with his promised sequel to his retelling of the classic Beauty & the Beast story.

He hadn't meant for it to end so cruelly in *The Beast of*

Brooklyn Heights, but his heart had been broken at the time. After reviewers and audiences, the world over had clamored for a sequel, Oliver had finally announced that it was in the works.

That had been a year ago. He figured he owed it to them, and to his characters. They deserved better than how he'd left them. The problem was simple, Oliver was stuck.

Writer's block, that galling game-stopper, that vexatious variable, had hit him hard. Oliver was simply unable to find the perfect end for the tale. He growled softly, careful of the non-supernaturals, the *normals* in the crowd.

He straightened his shoulders. He was no longer the sad young Bear, orphaned in his teens who'd remained solitary and penniless until he finally hit it big. But that was only after he'd arrived in the city to fulfill the destiny his mother had described to him when he was a young cub. After he'd met her and had his whole life turned upside down and inside out.

Oliver had left a part of him behind in Brooklyn Heights. In the wake of the worst heartbreak of his life. Even worse than having to grow up far too soon. He'd spent most of his adult life alone. Away from the Clan of his birth, and with no family of his own. What did he have now?

He had money. He had fame. And he clung to both desperately. Jaw clenched he straightened his shoulders. The tailored suit he wore was like armor to him. The absolute best money could buy, and he had tons of that these days. The vultures circling him could not harm him as long as he remained aloof and in control.

Being a successful composer, playwright, and screenwriter had its perks. He'd worked feverishly the past couple of years and had sold more stories than he'd been expecting. Hollywood loved him and wanted his input on several of their fantasy fairytale retellings. He was Broadway's baby as far as Chance was concerned, not that he enjoyed the moniker one bit.

Still, it allowed him some freedom, he admitted. Oliver could now afford the finer things in life and that included his privacy. He could have anything money could buy.

Unfortunately, it was true what they said. Money could not buy happiness. Neither his human side nor his beast would ever feel that again. The Bear inside him chuffed at the thought. But Oliver would not relent. He could make such a statement with absolute certainty these days.

"You'll have the pages, Chance. I just need some time. I'm going away to my cabin for a few weeks to finish it. Should be ready before the Easter holidays."

"Perfect. And I get it, Pax, sometimes a man needs a little quiet. Say, did you want to do a late dinner with Leandra and me?"

"Uh, no, I-" Oliver was having a hard time concentrating on Chance's words as reporters clamored for his attention.

"Okay, people, enough," Chance waved them away.

"It's fine," he growled.

A few of the crowd moved away from his snarling, but one form did not sway. Oliver blinked slowly. It couldn't be, he shook his head. Great. He was hallucinating.

The vultures were everywhere. Usually, he brought a woman with him to opening night as a sort of armor, but just lately his Grizzly was having a difficult time being around members of the opposite sex. His beast would tolerate no one getting close to him.

The last time he went out with a woman, his date had mistaken gratitude for an invitation. Oliver had to work way too hard to stop the animal from rising within him and flinging the forward female away. It simply wasn't worth the risk to himself or anyone else.

He looked at the throng and frowned hard. Had his eyes deceived him again? He could have sworn he saw, but no, it was impossible. She couldn't be there. That was twice now, he growled at himself.

"Damn it, do these people have no regard at all for privacy?"

"Come on Oliver, it's part of the job. You know that. Just look at them for a sec and wave, let them get their picture and be done with it," Chance nodded and smiled, and finally, Oliver turned his head to do the same.

They could snap their pictures, but the hell with smiling. It never ceased to amaze him how these fiends all looked the same with their ill-fitting rumpled clothes from hiding in corners and behind bushes to get photos for whatever rags would buy them.

Still, if it sold tickets, he owed that to Madoc, the stars, and the dozens of employees at the theatre. Shows ran for however long they were popular, and newspapers and bloggers helped spread the word.

"Look this way Mr. Pax!"

"Can we get a smile Pax?"

"Ollie?"

His head snapped in the direction of the softly whispered nickname that only one person in the world had ever had the gumption to call him.

"Teresa," he whispered.

Mate, his Bear roared.

"Ollie," she stood over a dozen feet away, but he heard her loud and clear among the shouting crowd.

Oliver's whole body tensed. Feelings he'd worked hard to suppress over the past two years threatened to erupt inside of him like a volcano. His Bear pushed to be let out, to do the things his human side wouldn't, like go to her side.

He watched as her jade green eyes filled with tears. It couldn't be her. Why here? Why now? Anger and hurt welled inside of him.

"Please, Ollie?"

"Pax, who is that woman?" Chance asked him, but Oliver couldn't answer.

"No one," Oliver said hardening his heart to her beauty and his beast's natural impulse to go to her.

The sound of her gasp was heart-wrenching, but he ignored it and her. Painful as it was, Oliver turned his back on the one woman the universe had created just for him. The only woman he'd ever loved and who'd thrown his love back in his face.

Yes, he turned his back on her, but not before he saw her reach out her hand as if to touch him. She retreated as if burnt and brought that very same appendage back to her lips in some vain attempt to try and hold in the sob that had already escaped.

"Pax?"

He shook his head at Chance. There were some things he simply would not discuss. Teresa Witherspoon was one of them. His breathing came deep and heavy as he tried to get control of his internally rampaging Grizzly Bear. He hardly noticed Chance lunge forward.

"Holy shit. Stop! Wait!" Chance yelled, but it was too late a warning.

Oliver turned in time to see the woman who'd broken his heart run from his cruel rejection and straight into oncoming traffic.

The sound of tires squealing on the wet asphalt and the grinding of brakes were nothing compared to the crunch of

Teresa Witherspoon hitting the windshield of a yellow cab right outside the theatre.

"No!" he roared as he ran over to her broken and blood-soaked body.

"Ollie," she whispered before closing her eyes.

"No. No. NOOOOOOO!"

"Someone call 911," Leandra's voice reached him, but he couldn't look at her or anyone else. His eyes were riveted to the pale face of the woman he held to his chest.

Blood soaked through his ten-thousand-dollar suit, but Oliver couldn't have cared less. The sounds of sirens reached him through the roaring inside his head.

He let go of her reluctantly so the EMT's could do their job, ready to walk away and follow when her hand reached out and grabbed his.

"Get in the back," yelled one EMT above the thunder.

"Go ahead, Oliver, Leandra and I will follow you there," said Chance.

"Yes," Oliver nodded.

The EMTs worked together feverishly hooking her up to all sorts of machinery and some kind of IV drip. Oliver had to fight to stop his Bear from snarling at the men. They were only doing their jobs.

He looked down at the pale hand gripping his so tightly before it suddenly went lax. That moment was the single most terrifying in his life. He felt as though he were in a trance, as if he wasn't really there.

"What is happening?" he asked trying hard not to let despair take him.

"We're losing her," one of them said, "is she your mate?" he added almost imperceptibly. Oliver gave a single nod in response.

"Then you might say something, anything to help bring

her back while we work on her, alright?" The soft glow of that one EMT's eyes told Oliver all he needed to know.

The man was a Shifter, like him. He understood the pain and the agony that came with losing a mate, but what he couldn't know was that Oliver had been dealing with that pain for a couple of years now. He'd thought himself immune to her, but he'd been a fool.

It was true, Oliver was the biggest damn fool in the world to think this woman did not matter to him anymore. His Bear roared inside of him and he felt his heart constrict in his chest as the men brought out the defibrillator.

That precious pale hand was so small in his, he wondered how he ever let her go. Her blood pressure dropped, the machine monitoring her heart let out a long single note, and then Oliver knew real pain.

"No! I can't lose her now! Do something!"

"We are. Clear!" yelled one of the strangers.

Oliver watched helplessly as the EMT's worked frantically to get her back. She couldn't turn up again in his life simply to die now. He wouldn't allow it. No, she had to wake up and answer for what she'd done. He needed an explanation. He deserved one.

To hell with all that, his Bear snarled. *Mate!*

"Teresa, come back, come back to me dammit, I won't watch you die!" he yelled, and felt wet tears streaming down his face without embarrassment.

Two years might have passed, but he remembered every single moment of their time together. The way she laughed at his jokes and clung to him during their lovemaking.

She'd been new to passion. A virgin when he'd met her. That precious gift she'd given to him and how he had savored it and her. Dammit! He couldn't watch her die. Not now.

So many nights he'd dreamt about her. The ghost of her had kept him awake for months on end. He'd written scores about it. Musicals and movies describing his longing and his hurt.

The critics called his unrequited love stories angsty and unfinished. He supposed they were. Just like him.

"Come on, Resa! Wake up, dammit! Fight, you fight and you tell me why you've come back now! Wake up!" he roared.

"We have a pulse," the Shifter EMT smiled and nodded his head.

"Thank God," Oliver breathed and pressed his forehead to hers.

Mate, chuffed his Bear.

CHAPTER TWO

Teresa's entire body felt as if she were on fire. Like that burning sensation of pins and needles in your back when you cough too hard or hold your breath for too long.

What happened? Where was she?

She opened her eyes and blinked against the harsh fluorescent lights. The acrid smells of cleaning detergent and disinfectant made her want to gag, but there was something in her mouth preventing her from doing so.

"Easy, don't fight the tube, it is helping you breathe," said a deep, rumbly voice next to her head.

It was familiar, and so welcomed she wanted to cry and smile at the same time. Her thoughts were hazy, even she recognized that. Teresa tried to move to see the owner of that voice, but she couldn't.

What the heck? A deep throbbing ache pulsed from her ribs and her shoulders. An accident of some kind? She recalled the sounds of wheels spinning on asphalt and the crunch of broken glass.

Crap. She blinked slowly, willing herself to calm. Then

he came into view, and her heart started pounding once more inside her chest as panic took hold.

Ollie.

Deep brown eyes so dark they sometimes looked black stared at her from a face so handsome and familiar, so loved and missed that she could hardly breathe. His hair was shorter and his beard longer now, but she would know him anywhere.

He'd gotten older, more cynical, but she was probably to blame for that. It didn't matter, he was still handsomer than any other man in the universe as far as she was concerned.

Oliver Pax. His name lit up inside her brain like a neon sign. It all came pouring back to her in a storm of memories overwhelming every other thought. She couldn't stop the echoes of the past from filling the space between her ears.

Two long years since she'd last seen him, lying asleep in the bed where they'd made the sweetest love and created a life he didn't know about.

Thomas! Her son. Their son. Teresa had to get back to him. She tried sitting up, but Oliver pressed her back into the bed with a firm, yet gentle hand on her shoulder.

"You can't move yet, Resa. You're hooked up to a million machines here. Calm down, okay? I'll call a nurse," he went to move but she grabbed his hand.

Just then a strange man and woman came into the room. Panic rose and once more she struggled to sit up, he quirked an eyebrow at her. His expression hard and curious. She couldn't blame him. Not after what she'd done.

"Oliver?" the woman said his name and ran to him.

She embraced him in a quick little hug that made the darkness inside of Teresa rise up in jealousy. No, she told the thing and furiously beat it back to the cell where she'd trapped it. She visualized the hard iron bars until the dark thing inside of her quieted once more.

"Pax, is she okay?" the man said.

He was handsome, she supposed, with neatly combed hair and an easy smile, but he had nothing on her Ollie. Except, he wasn't her Ollie anymore.

Yes, she could have had a life with him once, but she'd given that up in order to protect him. Not that he knew about any of that. It didn't matter now. Only Thomas did.

"She is awake," the woman had a nice face, and a pleasing smile, "we were so worried. I'm Leandra and this is my husband Chance. We work with Oliver. I found your purse in the street and brought it with me," she said, and held up the tattered canvas tote Teresa had been using as a pocketbook for some time now.

To think she'd once donned the latest in fashion trends. She'd had her choice of haute couture hanging in her closets and the shoes and accessories to match. Nowadays, it was thrift stores and garage sales for Teresa.

She didn't mind as long as that meant she had more for Thomas. Her sweet boy was growing like a weed these days. His solid little toddler body seemed to need new clothes and shoes every few weeks.

Thomas. Her boy needed her. It was why she'd sought out Oliver to begin with. She hated herself for the secret she'd kept for so long, but now she knew there was something wrong with her.

Something had finally risen after she'd escaped from her father's and Witherspoon Tech's strange experiments. She needed help protecting Thomas and who better than his father?

"I see our patient is awake," a man in a white coat came

in and she looked hard to see if she recognized him from her father's labs.

She couldn't be sure, so she waited seemingly complacent. The so-called doctor smiled and asked everyone to leave the room to which she violently shook her head.

"Oh, I think we'll stay," said the woman, Leandra, with a smile that didn't quite reach her eyes.

Teresa decided right then and there to like her. Oliver stood closer to her bed, and the man, Chance, mimicked his position on the other side of her. She watched the doctor and saw anger in his eyes before he placed a fake smile on his face once more.

"Alright then I will be right back with some medicine," he ducked out of the room.

The second he was gone, Teresa sat up and yanked the tube out of her mouth despite the cries of the three in her room. She coughed and held her throat. It would stop in a moment, another side effect of her father's madness. Teresa was a fast healer. Like magically fast.

"Teresa?" Oliver wore his concern on his sleeve and for that her heart swelled with a long since felt emotion.

"Ollie," she gasped, her voice rough from the tube, "we have to go now. That man is not a doctor. Have to leave."

"What?"

"I'm in trouble. Please," her eyes pleaded with him to believe her.

To her surprise he nodded his head and looked from her to his friend. Chance and Leandra nodded and the woman smiled at Teresa.

"Go, take her with you, Oliver. Get her to safety and then let us know where you are," Leandra said and started removing her coat. She handed it over to Teresa along with her jeans and a pair of white sneakers.

"I'll wear Chance's coat. You just put these on, here Chance give her your tie, she'll need it as a belt."

The slightly curvier woman giggled and helped Teresa don her haphazard outfit. It was perfect. She impulsively hugged the woman before leaving.

"Thank you," Teresa said.

"He's coming back, let's go the other way," Oliver grabbed her hand and pulled her along down the corridor.

Once outside, he flagged down a cab and closed the door.

"Where to?" the cabbie asked.

"High Falls Towers-"

"No, we have to go to 201-B Allen Street, please," she sat up and gave the cabbie the directions to the apartment she'd been sharing with a young would-be actress.

"Why there?"

"Ollie, there is a lot you don't know-"

"Oliver. My name is Oliver," he corrected her and her stomach flipped.

"Okay, Oliver then. Look, I have a lot to tell you. I don't expect you to just forgive and forget but believe me when I say I need your help," her voice cracked at the end and she bit the inside of her mouth to stop from crying.

She didn't expect pity, hell, she didn't even deserve it. But this was bigger than her. It was bigger than them both.

"Can you wait?" she asked the cab driver who nodded his head.

"Teresa, where are we going?"

"I have to get something first, then can you get me out of town?"

"Yes," he nodded. Just like that.

"How are you feeling?" Oliver squinted at her as she took the stairs to the second floor two at a time.

"I'm fine," she shrugged.

"You have five broken ribs and a fractured clavicle," he said.

"They must've been mistaken," she said.

"I saw the scans, Teresa," he said and grabbed her arm.

"I will explain, but we have to move fast. Please," she insisted.

She hated keeping it from him, but she needed to get to her son first. It wasn't fair to keep it a secret, the darkness inside her, even as it healed her quickly, was something that was growing and would soon take over. She couldn't risk hurting her son.

Oliver had to keep him safe. Besides, like father like son. Teresa knew Thomas was a Shifter like his dad. The boy already showed signs. Oliver could teach their boy how to control his own Bear.

Oliver had told her everything back when they were together. He'd confided his wondrous secret of being a Shifter when they were carefree and in love. Back before she'd known the truth about her father and his nefarious deeds.

"You seem *different*," he said and followed her down the hall.

"I know and I will explain, but first I think you need to prepare yourself," she started.

"For what?"

"Ollie, I have a-"

Before she could finish her sentence the door to the apartment burst open and the almost two-year old whirlwind also known as Thomas Pax came crashing into her legs, nearly toppling her to the ground.

"Mommy!!!" her boy shouted and rained a dozen sloppy

precious little kisses on her cheeks when she'd scooped him up.

"Hello, sweet boy," she rubbed her nose against his and winced a little as his very-big-for-his-age forty-pound body wriggled in her arms hitting any one of the bruises she had left from the accident.

"Mommy's late! Nancy sleepin'."

"She is? How did you know I was here?"

"Sniffed ya, Mommy," he giggled.

"You did, huh?" she smiled at her curly-haired son and breathed a sigh of relief that he was with her and safe.

"Teresa?" Oliver's near black eyes met hers and she knew he'd scented the truth without words.

"Mommy, who's the man?" Thomas whispered loudly as most children his age tended to do.

"Thomas, this is Oliver Pax."

"My name Pax. Thomas Pax!"

"Yes, it is, sweet boy. Oliver, this is Thomas. He's our son."

CHAPTER THREE

Oliver's chest squeezed painfully around that useless organ that dwelt inside. A son? He had a son.

Too many emotions to count raged through him as he took in the dark haired little boy who had the same brown eyes and stubborn chin as him. This was his boy, his son.

Our cub, corrected his Grizzly Bear, and all he needed was one sniff to scent the truth in both words.

He smelled the familiar deep pine forest scent that was his own with a bit of peaches and some sunshine thrown in. Oliver smiled. The small cub was his and he was a Shifter too.

He could scent the fur beneath the skin and even that was strange. Most Shifters did not have their first transformation until after puberty, but this young cub's seemed much closer than that.

"I need to get our bags from the closet, can you stay here with your Daddy?"

"Uh huh, hi Daddy," said Thomas.

He looked up at Oliver curiously. Fear and apprehension were both absent, which immediately had Oliver's previously unknown paternal pride soaring to ridiculous heights. The boy was brave. So fragile and new, his paternal instincts came rushing forward and regardless of what had happened in the past he knew he would do anything for his son.

"Hello, Thomas," he greeted his cub.

Not the bells and whistles, triumphant introduction of a prolific composer to his long-lost progeny, but what else could he say. A few minutes ago he hadn't even known the child existed.

"The bad men comin'?" the boy, *his son* asked.

His inner Grizzly snarled at the words. What bad men dared threaten his young? That could wait though.

Oliver crouched in front of his cub. He wanted the toddler to be able to look at the strange man who was his father, to see him eye to eye so that he could gauge the truth himself.

"Thomas, I promise no more bad men. I will protect you. Always."

"Mommy too?"

Oliver looked up and saw Teresa standing there, holding her breath. She placed the two suitcases she was holding on the floor and bent to scoop Thomas up before he had a chance to answer the boy.

"That's enough questions, buddy, come on," she said, and smiled brightly at the child despite the tears in her eyes.

"I'll get those," Oliver said and reached for the two small suitcases before Teresa could try to lift them.

Despite what she said about being fine, he saw her wince when she lifted their son. He stopped and swallowed. It was a momentous occasion after all. Those two small words were now suddenly a part of his vocabulary.

My son, he thought with wonder as he preceded the mother and cub down the hall.

Even though she would not let him answer Thomas's question, Oliver would always protect her and their cub with everything he had inside of him. That meant with all the strength of his Grizzly Bear.

The beast inside of him chuffed and grumbled at the idea that the two most important beings in the world to him, that his precious and newfound family, were in danger. He didn't know what they were running from, but that wasn't important. He would see them safe, then he would get answers.

Grrr.

After they'd reached his apartment, Oliver directed them to the parking garage and to his fully equipped black Range Rover. He was already packed for the trip up to his cabin deep in the woods behind Indian Lake in upstate New York.

"We're not going upstairs?" inquired Teresa, and Oliver just shook his head.

"It's a long ride, you might want this," he handed her a small travel pillow and blanket that he had in the trunk from the last time he'd driven up there with Terrence and Daisy.

Terrence was an exceptionally talented Broadway director, and one of Oliver's only friends along with Chance. He was also a Vampire and had recently mated a human woman by the name of Daisy who had a penchant for growing things. She'd been thrilled to come up to the cabin to explore the native flora, but in her delicate condition had required naps along the four-hour drive.

"Sleepy," mumbled Thomas who was already close to dozing in his mother's arms.

"Does he need a car seat?" Oliver stopped in his tracks.

"It's fine. This model has a built-in booster," she smiled.

It wasn't a coincidence that Oliver had bought Teresa's favorite car. It was one of those things he'd almost forgotten in their many silly little conversations they'd had about everything and nothing.

"He's big enough to sit in the booster with the seat belt on," she said softly.

Oliver held the door to the back of the SUV open while Teresa leaned down to open the booster then placed the precious cub on the plush leather interior. He watched as she competently buckled him in and checked to make sure he was secure before propping the pillow on the backpack he'd brought with him filled with his toys and things only a child would find important.

Teresa tucked a lock of thick glossy brown hair behind the child's ear and rubbed the lobe. He was so small and innocent. Clearly, she cared for him a great deal. He could see it in the way she touched his forehead and dropped a kiss on his plump cheek, then covered him with the fluffy fleece blanket Daisy had left behind. He was grateful now that she had.

Teresa moved to climb in next to Thomas, but Oliver stopped her with a hand on her elbow. Even that simple platonic touch was enough to make his Bear growl and his heart thump heavily inside his chest.

He wanted her, he realized, and accepted it for the fact it was. She was his one true and fated mate. Desire was a byproduct. He'd known it the second he'd spied her reading in the park the very first time. Fresh as a spring flower just ready to bloom, she'd stolen his heart, then she ran away with it. The cut of her betrayal was still raw despite the passage of time and he tightened his hold momentarily before releasing her.

"Sit in the front," he muttered the gruff order before turning his back on her.

Surprisingly, Teresa obeyed him. She took the long way around and eased into the passenger seat, wincing gingerly when she fastened her seatbelt over her ribs. They must still be bruised. The truth of her rather quick recovery bothered him as did the odd hint of something *other* in her natural peaches and cream fragrance.

"You want answers, I'm sure," she said in a quiet voice without any emotional inflection apparent.

How can she be so calm when my heart is beating like a thousand drums and my brain feels like it's about to explode?

He shook his head and started the vehicle. The tank was full and a small cooler with sandwiches and drinks was packed. It sat on the floor at her feet.

"Pass me a water, please," he pointed at the cooler and watched her fulfill his request slowly.

Shit. He'd forgotten her injury already.

"Sorry, I shouldn't have asked you to get that."

"No, it's fine," she handed him the bottle and he gestured for her to take one for herself, which she did.

She drank thirstily, finishing the entire thing before she pulled it from her plump pink lips. He'd been hypnotized by that bee-stung mouth of hers from the first. He knew from experience just how soft and warm those lips were. How they tasted like her scent, fresh peaches with sweet cream to be savored under a warm spring sun.

Oliver swallowed his water along with the bitterness of his memories. Whatever was going on, Teresa definitely owed him more than she'd said so far. He glanced in the rearview mirror at his sleeping son and his beast rumbled.

Mine.

Whether he meant the cub or the woman beside him, Oliver wasn't sure. He had the feeling his animal was laying claim to both. Unfortunately, he didn't know if he had it in him to be rejected again. He might not survive it this time around.

"He is my son."

It was a statement. Oliver waited a beat before looking at the woman who'd turned his world upside down then tore it to shreds when she'd left him with a single callously scrawled note.

"Yes. He is our son."

"When?"

"I think he was conceived the last time we," she swallowed, "uh, it was just after Christmas. Anyway, he was born early, the second of May."

"Shifter pregnancies are usually a few months less than normal ones. Did you have any difficulty?"

"At first, you see I didn't know I was pregnant, and my father, well," she was grasping her hands tightly together.

The scent of her anxiety was making his own beast want to hunt something down and kill it, whatever it was that had made her so afraid. That sounded fine to his Bear. Hunt, kill, protect.

"What? I knew so little about your home life. Other than the fact you're the heiress to the great man Mathias Witherspoon himself-"

"My father is not a great man," she said angrily, "my father is a madman who experimented on his own child. He injected me with something, I don't know what it was, but it's bad, Oliver."

"What? Teresa what are you saying?" he gripped the steering wheel tightly in his hands.

"Witherspoon Tech isn't just making applications for medical research and development. They have a research facility, a secret one. And I don't know how, but my father knows about your kind."

"What do you mean? Did you tell him?"

"No," she gasped, "I would never betray you like that."

"Oh no? You left me, Teresa, I can't think of any worse betrayal than that," he sneered before he could stop himself.

"I know. I don't expect you to believe me , but he threatened to put you in a cage. I couldn't allow that, Oliver. And no, I didn't tell him, he had video of you in the woods."

"What?"

"Our one camping trip we took out of the city. He had me followed. Look, he knows and he did something to me after I left you, I let him do it. I wanted to protect you, but I am so scared now. Whatever he did, it was bad, Ollie, I mean Oliver," her frightened words reached his ears over the hum of the engine.

"What are you saying exactly?"

"I have something bad inside of me, Ollie," she whimpered and cleared her throat, "I have it locked down right now, and yes, I know I sound like a crazy person, but I am telling you the truth. I'm scared, Oliver, for Thomas' sake. I don't know if I can keep it under control much longer," she whispered that last bit.

Oliver turned his head briefly to look at her as they made their way towards the bridge that would take them out of Manhattan. Her ashen face was like a knife to his heart, as was the stoic way she swallowed her tears. She looked at him with her head held high. She always was brave when he'd expected her to cower. Like the first time he'd shown her his Bear in an effort to stop her from seeing him.

Oliver thought he was doing the noble thing, but she'd walked right up to his thousand-pound animal and petted him like a dog. Stupid Bear went belly up for her. Even now, she still was brave, despite the fact he didn't have a clue what she was talking about.

She faced him like a stowaway about to walk the plank, he thought as he watched resignation leak into her gaze. She clenched her jaw, eyes darting to the cub who sat sleeping in the rear seat before returning to him again.

"I won't bother to explain why I did what I did. It's enough that you trust me so far as to take us out of the city and away from Witherspoon Tech. Some of my father's men spotted me this week and I can't be sure but that ER doc didn't seem legit," she shrugged.

"There was something off about him," Oliver muttered and turned his head to the street in front of him.

It was nearing on two o'clock in the morning, but he was wide awake. She'd given him a lot of food for thought, and there was his Bear to deal with the animal couldn't understand his reticence. All the beast knew was that he had his mate within reach and he wanted to hold on tightly to her.

He tried to refocus on the reasons he should stay away, to keep his heart distant, but it was a losing battle. Even a Grizzly couldn't take on the Fates. Oliver inhaled a deep breath, allowing the subtle sweetness of her scent to invade his senses.

He knew the exact moment Teresa succumbed to sleep in the quiet interior of the vehicle. All tension left her bruised body, and she slumped away from him, her head resting on the cool window. She looked so small and tired.

Oliver frowned, but he made no move to touch her. Still, he didn't want her uncomfortable. Concern got the best of him, and he took off his suit jacket and draped it over her, keeping one hand on the wheel at all times. After all, he was hauling precious cargo.

The fact that he was a father astounded him. Pride, love, sadness, and anger warred within him for dominance. He was sad that he'd missed even a second of his sweet little cub's life. He was angry that Teresa had run from him, but he wasn't quite sure if that anger was directed at her or the monsters, real or imaginary, that she was still running from.

He decided to settle on the love he felt for Thomas. His heart swelled with the irrational feeling, almost impossibly so. He felt like the Grinch at the end of the story, when his heart grew so large it burst through the measuring slide. How could he love someone so much that he just met?

Easy, his Bear answered, *ours*.

His feelings toward the cub's mother were a bit more complicated. Teresa was his fated mate, there was no denying that, but it was impossible to just forget the hurt and pain she'd caused him. Was he big enough to let all that go? He supposed he would have to wait and see what the rest of her explanation was when they got to the cabin, and what her plans for the future were.

Mate, said his Grizzly Bear.

The animal inside of him didn't seem to care about the past, only that she was with him now, and his furry beastie had no intentions of letting her go a second time around.

Mine.

CHAPTER FOUR

Oliver stopped at the last gas station and minimart before they reached the mountain and his log cabin. It was just after five o'clock in the morning and the air was nippy but typical for early spring.

"Resa," he called her by the nickname he'd given her back when they were together, and watched in fascination as she slowly blinked those creamy jade green eyes up at him with a small smile on her face.

That soft expression lasted all of a few seconds before the hard mask fell once more and she shot up too fast. He felt guilty when she winced against the pain such a fast movement had surely sent through her healing bones.

"Are we there yet?" she asked.

"No, I just wanted to ask if you needed anything? I am stopping for some perishables before we head up to my cabin."

"A cabin? Oh, um, I have some money," she started rummaging through her jeans, and shame welled up inside of him.

"I have money," he said, "just tell me what you need."

"Thomas likes orange juice and milk, um, eggs, bacon, sausage, and wheat bread. Peanut butter and honey with bananas," she whispered.

"That's my favorite," Oliver said and watched in amazement at the pink blush that spread across her face.

Still lovely after everything that had happened, he thought. Without meaning to, Oliver reached out with his hand and touched her wan cheek. His heart pounded with feeling as she pressed her soft, warm skin against his palm. He narrowed his eyes at her and, as if he'd been burned, he took his hand away.

"I'll get everything," he said and cleared his throat, "lock the doors till I get back," he left the car running just outside the entrance to the minimart.

It was still early and no one else was there, but he wanted Teresa and their son in his line of vision at all times. Oliver entered the tiny, but adequate store and waved hello to Mr. Barad, the owner and proprietor of both the station and the small minimart. He walked down the store's four aisles gathering supplies, stopping suddenly at a small stand displaying a variety of cheap but cute children's toys.

He pursed his lips before grabbing a couple of plastic play cars and some coloring books and crayons. He added two gallons of milk, three cartons of fresh squeezed orange juice, and as many packages of butter, eggs, bacon, and sausage that he could fit in his basket. He also grabbed some bags of salad, broccoli, carrots, onions, potatoes, tomatoes, and peppers. A boy needed his veggies.

Oliver had plenty of peanut butter and honey at the cabin already. Along with other non-perishables he used for cooking. At the checkout counter, he added four loaves of sliced wheat bread to finalize his order.

"Will that be all?" Mr. Barad asked as he started ringing up the items.

Oliver nodded and took out some cash, for some reason a little voice inside of him told him to forego paying with his credit card. Whatever. He grabbed his bags and walked to the back of his Range Rover waiting for the telltale click of the lock.

He settled the bags safely inside the spacious trunk, snug against their luggage and the cardboard box containing his work. He'd forgotten he was heading out to the cabin to finish the score for *Where Beauty Lives*.

"How much longer is it to your place?" Teresa asked.

"About forty minutes. My cabin is just behind the lake."

"Are there lots of people around?"

"Hmm? No. I like my privacy. There's a woman who lives up there year-round. Her home is about a fifteen-minute walk through the woods from my place. Everything else would take over half an hour by foot and longer by car."

"I'm sorry we're intruding on your privacy, Oliver."

"I have a son, Teresa, he is no intrusion. I want to get to know him."

"I see. Well, thank you, it means a lot."

"We will figure something out. I have a lawyer who handles my contracts and I am sure he can recommend a family lawyer to come up with some kind of custody agreement-"

A sob tore from her throat, and he looked up in shock to see her face buried in her hands. Noise from the backseat had his eyes glance to see Thomas stirring. Teresa must have heard it too because she covered her mouth tighter and slowed down her gasping.

"Mommy?"

"Yes, honey?" she answered the cub with false brightness, but Oliver still gave her points for trying.

Damn. He was a callous ass for bringing up custody. Especially when that wasn't what his Bear wanted him to say at all.

"You sad, Mommy?"

"No, honey boy, of course not. Look outside, see all the trees," she distracted their sweet cub who *ooohed* and *aaahed* for the next few minutes while playing *I Spy* with his mother.

The bags under her eyes and frown lines around her mouth, though taking nothing from her beauty, they also did nothing to appease his guilt. Oliver felt like an even bigger douchebag now for bringing up lawyers. His Bear grunted angrily inside him.

This was new territory for him, but he supposed it was for her as well. He made a mental note to apologize once they were settled and turned his attention to the narrow road that led to his cabin.

He'd purposely had it built into the landscape to discourage random stalkers, and yes, he did have some, from trying to find him. The address was unlisted, buried beneath several aliases and corporations so as to be untraceable to Oliver.

What could he say? He was a Bear who appreciated solitude. The air was nippy for spring, but it was to be expected at this altitude. Still, he hoped Teresa had packed appropriately.

Hell. It was thoughts like that one there that was going to wreak havoc in his life. When was the last time he'd cared about someone other than himself?

Oliver growled, ignoring her questioning stare, and turned into the semi-circle driveway. There were still patches of snow on the rocky ground. Combined with the buds on the trees, it looked as if mother nature had yet to make up her mind on what season it was. Typical for the Northeast, he supposed.

He'd worked with the architect on the design for the log cabin so that it would be inconspicuous and yet maintain the standard of luxury he was newly accustomed to. What could he say? Even Grizzlies liked their creature comforts.

"Wow," Teresa gasped as she took in the rustic looking two-story structure.

"I need to unlock the door, then I'll get the bags," he said and exited the vehicle.

Oliver had the latest state-of-the-art tech in security systems. *Draco Fortis* made the best. The company was owned and operated by a rare Dragon Shifter with exceptional skills and powers that he infused into all of his designs. The Falk brothers also happened to be fans of Oliver's work and the youngest, Nikolai, had installed the system himself just to get a chance to meet him. It was flattering and he welcomed the opportunity to visit with the unique and rare Dragon.

Oliver opened the sleek security pad that was hidden under a cut-out piece of log like the rest of the entire exterior, and he pressed his thumb to the reader before entering a secret passcode. After that, he used a standard key to unlock the massive wood door. Once inside, he activated the smart cabin using the touchscreen that was recessed into the wall.

Immediately, his generator started and electricity began to hum throughout the building. He was proud to say he'd also utilized wind and solar panels that stored energy into backup batteries to give power to the cabin. Oliver quickly pressed commands to start the central heat and he lit the fireplace, while switching the lights on. He swallowed nervously.

A woman, not any woman, *Teresa Witherspoon*, his runaway mate was about to enter his home away from home and oddly enough, he wanted her to like it. He straightened his shoulders and shook his head. What the hell was wrong with him? He walked back to the SUV, nodding at her to go in and went to the back to begin unloading the bags.

He tried not to notice the curve of her shapely body as she bent and took Thomas out of his seat. He was definitely sick for taking pleasure in her rounded bottom in her condition. His chest rumbled and he shushed his inner Bear.

"Mommy, forest!" the cub laughed and pointed at the tall pine trees and a single red cardinal that peeked out at him from one of the limbs.

"Yes, baby," she said and held his hand while he navigated the three steps to the open front door, slowly and carefully, "Thomas, easy does it," she said when he tried to run.

"Hungry," he said and rubbed his tummy.

"Alright, now let's sit at the table and I'll get you something to eat," Teresa spoke to him gently and he approved.

Oliver listened to the cue and grabbed the grocery bags first. He walked into the kitchen and almost tripped at what he saw there. Teresa settling Thomas on one of the tall counter chairs and licking her thumb to wipe a smudge from his nose. He snorted.

"What?" she asked mid-swipe.

"Nothing," he smirked, "it's just such a mom thing to do."

"Oh," she grinned back, "sorry."

"This Mommy," Thomas said and tilted his cherubic face to the side as if questioning Oliver's sanity.

"Yes, Thomas that is your Mommy. Do you know who I am?"

"Daddy," he bit his lip and waited, uncertain of Oliver's response.

"That's right," he said and crouched down to eye level with the boy, "I am your father."

Oliver watched as the boy cocked his head to the other side and his brown eyes deepened to near black. Oliver heard the chuff and whine of the child's young Bear and his own animal rose to respond to his cub for a brief poignant second. But how could that be?

His eyes darted to Teresa's and he saw her biting her lower lip. She was scared, that was obvious, and he wanted to snarl and roar once again to protect her.

"*Grisle* Bear likes you," Thomas said in a whisper.

"Grizzly, Thomas, it's Grizzly Bear, and that's good cause I like him too," Oliver said patiently.

"Hungry, Mommy, want dippy eggs," he blinked up at his mother, his Bear momentarily pushed aside.

"Me too," Oliver winked and stood, turning to Teresa who had started unpacking the groceries.

"Is it alright if I put these away and make something?"

"Of course, make yourself at home. I'll get the rest of the things."

Oliver vaguely registered the background noise of Teresa cooking in his kitchen. That was a marvel in and of itself, but he was distracted by another obvious and unusual truth.

Thomas, his cub, was a Shifter like him. Now, typically Shifters did not experience their first transformation until puberty. The child couldn't be more than two-years old, though age was difficult to tell in a Shifter baby since they grew more rapidly than normal children. Still, his Bear was very near to the surface. The boy could possibly have his first change a lot sooner than was usual.

He needed to call Jennifer. The Owl Shifter woman was the oldest creature he knew at over six-hundred years, though she didn't look a day over thirty. She lived in the forest near his cabin year-round and he knew her to be connected to some secret Shifter agencies that worked with keeping their secret from being outed to the rest of society.

Jennifer would know just how rare a thing it was for a young cub to be so close to his Bear, and she could possibly tell Oliver what to do. Besides, he could use other advice as well. Like on what he should do with Teresa. Plus, he'd brought the supplies she'd asked him for so that was a good excuse to call her for a visit. Maybe they could all go. Thomas would like to walk through the woods, he was sure.

The image the thought conjured up made his chest swell. Oliver had been alone so long, but now he had something he'd only ever dreamed of. A family.

That is, he had a son for certain, but whether or not Teresa would want to stick around was an unknown. Could he trust her even if she said she would stay?

Mate, his Bear once more supplied the answer, but Oliver was still unsure.

CHAPTER FIVE

"I finished washing the dishes and pans from breakfast, and Thomas is taking a nap in the bedroom you suggested. I thought, maybe now we could talk?" Teresa had spent an extra fifteen minutes washing the dishes just to build her courage to approach him.

Gosh, he was so handsome. More so now than he'd been back when she had first known him. Oliver Pax, the man himself, was as tall and wide as ever. Big as a house with taut muscles cording his enormous frame, smooth skin, usually bronzed from his time outdoors, was still a little on the pale side from the long, harsh winter they'd experienced.

He wore his beard close-cropped but thicker and longer than before, and his dark hair was shorter. He used to keep it a bit more shaggy, but she supposed that was more from it not mattering to him at the time. He looked more polished now.

His teeth were white and straight, and his chiseled features more emphasized by the expensive new hair-do. It was obvious he had become a success, even if she hadn't read all about him in every article and blog she could get her hands on over the past two years.

But his eyes are still the same, she thought as she inhaled the deep woodsy scent that she'd always attributed to him. Those rich brown orbs resembled freshly ground coffee beans with a dash of magical sparkle thrown in. Whenever his Bear was close to the surface they darkened impossibly so, to near black but they were not cold like the word implied. They were rich and warm, like molten dark chocolate.

Sigh. Teresa had given up her virginity staring into those bottomless velvet brown pools. She'd always known he was different, special somehow. Just like she'd always known she would love him until the day she died.

Oh, Oliver, her heart squeezed painfully in her chest. Looking into his now cold eyes, she couldn't help but remember how it used to be. How they'd once glittered in the darkness full of passion and love for her. She'd felt so safe, so cared for when she was in his arms. When he told her his secret she'd cried tears of joy. Just knowing real magic existed in this sometimes cruel world had given her so much hope.

Hope that she could end the nightmare that was her homelife. Her father had gone from distant and cold to intrusive and cruel once she'd started dating Oliver. She tried, oh how she tried, to keep it from him, but the man had her followed on more than once occasion.

She had to tell Oliver the truth now. All of it. She had no other choice. Thomas's life depended on it. Swallowing back her fears, she took one last look at the closely guarded expression on his gorgeous face. How many nights had she gone to bed sobbing into her pillow, tears in her eyes and pictures of him floating around in her head? It didn't matter now. Only Thomas mattered.

"Well?" he looked up from the sheet music in his hands.

The sight of Oliver writing music was nothing new. He seemed to always be working back in Brooklyn Heights and she used to love watching him. Amazed that he'd tolerated her presence while he captured the beautiful music in his brain on paper and recordings. There was none of that forbearance in him now. She shivered at the sharp note in his voice.

His eyes flashed behind her, concern on his face, and she warmed to him once more. It was obvious he was worried about their son, obvious he cared for their sweet baby as she'd always known he would.

Wow. She'd never expected to be able to even think those words much less say them. She inhaled a deep breath allowing the familiar forest scent of him to fill her nostrils. She opened her mouth slowly, taking the chance to utter those words aloud. Finally.

"Our son is special, Oliver, he's growing very fast, much more advanced than any human children," she watched him swallow down that fact, "he is bright and strong, and so very precious to me. You have to know I would do anything, hell, I would die to protect him."

"Teresa," he started, but she didn't allow him to finish the thought, she used the moment to take the chair across from him.

"I know this is not easy for you, Oliver. Believe it or not, it isn't easy for me either, but I need to say it. What I am about to tell you is going to sound mad, and you may not want to believe it, but I swear on my life it's the truth," she closed her eyes for a moment, the thing inside of her was riding her hard, and she had to work even harder to shut it down.

"I heard some of your story, Teresa, and I suppose it is only fair to warn you before you go down this road that Shifters like me can pick up on certain things with our supernaturally enhanced senses, like emotions, heightened pulse, even a rise in blood pressure," he quirked one eyebrow as he spoke, and Teresa couldn't help but think he was cute when he was being all arrogant.

Sigh. She'd been talked down to most of her life by one man or another. It was one reason she'd fallen so hard so fast for Oliver. He didn't treat her like an idiot. Until now.

"In other words," she looked right into his deep chocolate-colored eyes, "I shouldn't bother lying, is that it?"

"That's right," he said in a gravelly voice.

God, how she missed that about him. Oliver had the deepest, sexiest voice she'd ever heard. Especially when his Bear was pushing him as his majestic beast surely was now. She could only imagine why. The animal probably hated her for her abandonment. The very thought brought a stab of pain straight through her heart.

"I didn't know it then, but back when we were seeing each other my father was having me followed."

"You said that, but why would he do that?"

"A million reasons I suppose, but mainly to control me," she swallowed.

It was difficult to reveal this side of her life to him. Back then, she'd brushed aside all his inquiries about her home life, choosing to remain firmly in the comfort of his presence. It was so much better than thinking about her father and his maniacal attempt to control every aspect of her life.

"He found out, Ollie," she slipped, calling him by the nickname she'd given him back when he used to smile at her, before she left him thinking their relationship had been some trifle when in reality it had meant the world to her. Ollie she wanted to still be able to call him that. Her Ollie. But he'd corrected her that morning. He wasn't her Ollie anymore. He was Oliver.

The flare of his nostrils and slight widening of his eyes made her own breath catch in her throat, but by the time she blinked that look was gone. Maybe she'd imagined it.

Teresa would give anything for him to look at her the way he used to even if just for a moment. She closed her eyes and shook away the silly wish. She needed to remain focused on what she had to say.

Lord knew, she wouldn't get through this if she started thinking about all her regrets and longings. There were just too many and too much time had passed for that. She had Thomas to consider now. With that in mind, Teresa took a fortifying breath and moved on.

"Witherspoon Tech has been working in collaboration with some secret organization, I don't know what they are called, but I found messages signed or not signed exactly, but stamped with the image of a beetle on the bottom."

"What are you talking about?"

She huffed out a breath in frustration. The truth was she didn't have enough information on all the nefarious deeds of her father, but she knew it was bad. The fact that he had never stopped hunting her and her son, that he wanted to put sweet Thomas in a cage, frightened her more than anything else in the world.

"My father is into something truly evil, Oliver. He wants to study Shifters, and not for anything good. After the last night I spent with you, his men grabbed me just outside your apartment when I'd gone to catch a taxi. They brought me to him and he was horrible. He threatened you," her voice cracked as she lost herself in the memory.

Her father's steel eyes glittered at her wildly in the confines of his home office. Unfamiliar in his rage and revulsion, Teresa recoiled each time he raised his hand. He slapped her hard across her face and she tasted blood inside her mouth. She'd bitten the inside of her cheek with that last hit. Teresa begged him to stop, cowering on the floor in confusion at his apparent hatred of his only child.

"You little slut! How could you bed an animal! Just like your mother. You're no Witherspoon!"

"Father, please!"

She'd cried and begged. He did stop hitting her, but then he did something much worse. Nodding at someone behind her, Teresa found herself soon bound to a chair and forced to write a note to Oliver callously ending their relationship.

Afterwards, he had her taken to a secret lab where his henchmen took her blood and gave her a series of injections. Once she discovered her pregnancy, she was able to bribe one of the guards to release her. All she had to do was give the man the numbers to one of her father's bank accounts. After that, she ran.

"I couldn't go back to you, he would have been watching. I had to protect you and the life growing inside of me," Teresa blinked at the paper towel that was thrust in front of her face.

She'd been so lost in the memory that she didn't even realize she'd been crying. Oliver was kneeling beside her. His concerned expression made the tears fall harder, and she bit back a sob.

"Teresa, I don't know what to say," he began, and she nodded covering her face.

"I know you don't believe me, but I swear, he made me

write the letter, he told me he would kill you otherwise. He had pictures, Ollie, of you and your Bear, he was going to blackmail you and expose you," she cried harder, "then when I knew I was pregnant I had to get away from him. I don't know what he did to me, but there is something inside me now. Something bad. I can't let it out. If something happens to me and my father gets his hands on our baby who knows what he will do. He wants Thomas. He's tried to take him before, but I can't let that happen. You have to help, please, even if you don't believe me. You have to protect our son," she begged, foregoing all pride in her fight to save her son.

"Easy, easy, I believe you," he looked at her hard for a moment then tugged her into the familiar warmth of his powerful embrace, "I got you, Resa," he murmured and she clung to him.

"Thomas?"

"I have you both. He's my son, I will protect him. I have money now, power, connections, I'm a Grizzly Bear for fuck's sake and if anyone tries to mess with my son or his mother, that person will die," he vowed.

"Ollie," she breathed as relief and something else inside her began to take flight.

The feeling took off and lit up like fireworks. It felt good, right, being in his arms. Safe and protected. She breathed in his scent and clung to his strong capable shoulders. Teresa was finally home.

CHAPTER SIX

"Resa," Oliver squeezed her tight in his arms and nuzzled her cheek.

He turned slightly so that they were facing each other. They were so close that he could see the tear drops that clung to her dark blond lashes and his reflection in her creamy jade eyes. Oliver pressed her even closer still.

She was so beautiful. Even more so now that she'd matured. Her lovely lithe body had filled out in wondrous ways that both animal and man were dying to explore.

Shit. If he went down that road, he'd never find his way back. But right then, Oliver and his Bear did not give a damn. He wanted her. Wanted to feel her soft submission under his searching lips. Wanted to taste her peaches and cream scent on his tongue and swallow it down.

"Ollie," she said his name unconsciously swaying closer.

The scent of her sweet arousal reached him and he growled softly in response. She was hypnotizing him all over again, and right then he didn't care, wouldn't fight it. He wanted it and her, that sweet oblivion only she could give him. Oliver's heart thudded inside his chest.

Mine, growled his Bear.

He cupped her face in his hands, wondering at the way she turned into his touch, and the soft rumbling sigh that escaped her plump pink lips. Need flowed through him, an unstoppable tide. Why should he fight it?

Oliver made up his mind. He wouldn't go into this blindly this time, but now he had something else to fight for. His son. The child they had made out of love, yes love, he realized and believed it with everything in him.

This woman ripped out his heart once, but here she was begging him for help. It hurt to see her humbled and frightened. He wanted her strong and safe, and with him, always. Fate had given them another chance, and Oliver was going to take it and hold it with both hands.

He dipped his head, ready to take the first step. Teresa's eyes flashed and he growled in response to the desire he saw there. Their noses bumped, and he smiled, it had been playfully awkward the first time too.

Memories of how good it was tried to force their way into his mind, but he pushed them back. He didn't want to think about the past anymore. He only wanted to concentrate on the now.

"Resa," he said her name once more and carefully lifted her face to his, then he kissed her.

His temperature went from normal to boiling in that instant. Shifters tended to run a little hotter than *normals*, but even he felt the sizzle. She was right there with him, her skin was on fire under his searching hands and lips.

So hot. So good.

Her peaches and cream flavor burst on his taste buds, sending ripples of desire zipping up and down his spine, straight to his groin. She moaned and wrapped her arms around his back, pressing her soft breasts firmly against his chest. He could feel the bite of her pebbled nipples through their combined shirts and the animal grunted, wanting a closer touch.

This was a not just lust, it was mating fever. Oliver recognized it, reveled in it, and deepened their shared kiss. He delved into the hot cavern of her mouth with his tongue until he found hers. He sucked on it briefly, wanting to swallow down every single drop of her sweet flavor.

"Ollie," she moaned and slid off the chair.

She practically leapt off the chair with her legs wrapped tightly around him. Grunting, he caught her and held her to him, using minimal strength to stand. He lifted her up, cupping the firm globes of her ass, and walked them over to one of the sturdy log walls.

Oliver pressed into her core, allowing her to feel just how much he wanted her. Cock throbbing, pulse racing he kissed her deeper and ran his hands over her curvaceous form. She was so damned sumptuous. Every nuance and angle seemed to fit him like a glove.

"Mm, I'm bigger than I was," she whispered almost apologetically, and his Bear roared.

"You're perfect for me," he grunted, cupping her ripe breasts which were in fact larger than he remembered.

A result of having gone through childbirth, he supposed and his heart ached for the loss of time between them, but he didn't want to think about that just then. Oliver wanted to live in the moment like the cavalier poets she'd once relished. He wanted to stop time and dive right into the depths fully and completely with her.

"Bed," he said, and she nodded. That was all the consent he needed.

Oliver took the stairs to his master bedroom and dropped her gently on the bed. He was stunned for a moment. How many times had he dreamed of this moment? Of having her in his bed? Sure, he'd thought about exacting his revenge on this woman who had broken his heart and threatened to drive his Bear insane, but those thoughts were quickly fleeting. Mostly, he just dreamt of having her back.

And here she was, but this was no dream. This was real. Teresa was here in his bed, and revenge was the last thing on his mind. She bit her lip and looked at him, then, as if she'd come to some firm decision. Teresa sat up, eyes heavy-lidded with lust, she tore her shirt off, then her pants revealing every glorious inch of her lush body to his greedy eyes.

Oliver's dick throbbed as he took in her mouthwatering curves in the simple flower printed bra and panties she wore. Following suit, he stripped himself quickly.

He tumbled into the bed with her, growling softly as their lips met. A few maneuvers had them both fully naked and Oliver settled his body between her two soft thighs.

"Ollie," she whimpered, another wave of her arousal filled his nostrils.

His Grizzly Bear rose up inside of him and Oliver took one long look at her face before he pressed the head of his cock into her hot, slick entrance. Oh yes, she was more than ready for him, just as snug and tight as he remembered.

"Oh God, Ollie," she moaned and clung to his shoulders.

Oliver flexed his hips, trying hard not to lose it right then and there. So damn tight, so good. Perfect.

"Relax for me, sweet," he murmured kissing her again until he felt her muscles loosen their hold.

He was a big man, a big Bear. Even though they had done this before, it had clearly been a long time for her. Oliver had to go slowly, carefully. He would never willingly hurt her. He knew her body could take him, she just had to relax, and accept all of him into her hot, slick, velvety channel.

"S'good," she moaned, and he could feel her rising desire as it matched his own.

He looked down at her heavy-lidded eyes and dipped his head to capture her mouth. He thrust his tongue deep, mimicking the movement of his hips. Slow, steady at first, then faster and harder. Oliver's body was slick with sweat, his heart raced as he quickened the pace. This was crazy. They should have talked, but what did Shifters need with words when he could say it all with his body?

Mate, his Bear pushed him to mark her.

No, he shushed the beast.

This was not for the Bear. Not yet. This was for them. For him and Teresa. They needed this release, this closeness. Their relationship was too complicated for another rushed mating bite.

Still, even without the ritual biting, he could feel their *matebond* renew between them. He recognized the subtle difference, the new changes in her, and even though he didn't quite understand them, it did not matter. Oliver knew she had told him the truth earlier. He trusted her, in spite of their past. And he wanted her. Then. Now. Always.

"Ollie!" Teresa groaned his name and dragged her nails down his back.

He hissed in a sharp breath, the sting of her scratching hurt so good. His animal loved it. Her walls tightened around him, and her pussy rippled as she groaned her pleasure. She gripped his cock like a vise as she abandoned herself to the ecstasy only he could give her. He was her mate, there would be no other who could touch her this way.

The knowledge made it all the sweeter as he pumped harder and faster, chasing his own orgasm until he felt it erupt from him like a volcano. Arrogant, maybe, but he had right to be. Teresa was his.

"Mine," he couldn't stop the possessive word from spilling from his lips, just as he spilled his seed deep into her womb.

The idea that even then they could have created a life made his Bear chuff in approval. He wanted family. Wanted Thomas and all of their future cubs. Wanted Teresa now more than he ever had before.

Her eyes were still closed, mouth open as she tried to catch her breath. Oliver simply stared for a moment. With her blonde hair spread out over the gray comforter like a halo, she looked ethereal. He'd always thought there was something angelic about her appearance, so sweet and precious. Unearthly, and almost unattainable, but not for him. She'd let him have her.

"It's only ever been you," she said as if answering his unspoken question.

"I know," he kissed her softly and slid from her heat, missing the warmth immediately.

The sound of little footsteps had both of them jumping up, and Oliver had his pants back on before the little cub could wander into their room.

"Mommy," Thomas was still rubbing his eyes so he missed the look between the two adults as she donned one of Oliver's t-shirts and stood up to walk to him.

"Hey, baby," she dropped to her knees and hugged their son.

Thankfully, the shirt fell past her thighs though at his tender age he would hardly notice his mother's nudity. Besides, Shifters were not prudes about things like that.

Being naked was natural and made transforming from one skin to another easier and less messy.

He watched mother and cub kneeling together and Oliver's heart threatened to burst at the picture they made. Were they really both his? He listened to the pleasant conversation the two were having and watched as she drew the cub along with her out into the hall with a wave for him to follow. Oliver did with wonder in his heart.

Teresa brought the boy to the large guest bathroom on the first floor and started the water. The bathtub was massive but not too large for so young a Bear. It was done in natural creams and blues, but suddenly Oliver wished he'd had something fun painted on the walls. He'd made a mental note to have an artist come and do the bathroom and guest room over as Thomas' private rooms. Perhaps he had a favorite character or movie they could use as models. So much he didn't know about his cub.

"What's wrong?" Teresa broke his reverie and he looked into her worried eyes.

"Nothing, I was just wondering if he had a favorite book or TV show?"

"Oh, no favorites yet, but he does like it when I sing to him. Mostly show tunes or movie theme songs," she shrugged and began humming one of the numbers he'd written for a big cartoon movie that had released last year.

Thomas clapped and splashed in the water and Teresa winked at Oliver. He felt his Bear rumble happily inside of him. She was teasing him, but there was truth to her statement. Also, that meant she'd been keeping tabs on him.

"Toys, Mommy?" Thomas asked.

"Oh, buddy, I'm sorry I forgot the bath toys," she frowned, but Oliver interrupted.

"Actually, I have something young master Thomas

might like," he said and went to retrieve the toy cars he'd bought at the minimart.

"Vroom!" Thomas squealed with delight when he saw the tiny plastic cars things and Oliver looked at Teresa for approval.

"That was nice of Daddy," she smiled, "now, settle down you don't want to slip," she chided the cub who immediately started racing the two cars through the bubbles on the side of the bath.

"He likes them," Oliver grinned and Teresa walked over to stand by him.

He immediately tucked her into his side as they stood together and simply watched their son play. Nothing could describe the happiness that welled inside of him at seeing his heathy, mischievous lad splashing water over the side of the bath and giggling wildly at his mother's faux chiding.

"Thank you," she whispered to Oliver.

"They're just little things," he shrugged.

"To you maybe, but to him it's a lot. We haven't had much, but I did my best for him, Oliver," he caught the hitch in her words and he frowned.

"Hey, I know you did, I would never say otherwise. It's going to be alright now, I got you both."

Looking to make sure Thomas was safe for the moment, Teresa tugged him out into the hallway. She turned to face him and he could tell by the way she squared her shoulders she'd made up her mind about something.

"So, I just want to make sure you will take care of Thomas?"

"What? Of course, I know he's my son-"

"Cause I've decided to turn myself in to my father and Witherspoon Tech in exchange for them leaving you and Thomas alone."

"What?" he whispered barely holding on to his rage.

"It's the only way," she pleaded, but he wasn't hearing it.

"No, Teresa. Just no. I let you go once. I won't do it again."

"But-"

"You came to me this time, Teresa."

"For him. So you can keep him safe," she said.

"It's not enough. I love him so much, but I need you too, now do you trust me?"

"Of course, I do," she said and he could tell from the misery rolling off her that she only wanted to protect them both. It touched him, but it made him crazy all the same.

"I got this, Resa," he said.

"Alright," she answered and leaned in, just a breath away from his lips.

"Mommy!" Thomas called, and the two adults jumped apart and raced back to the bathroom just in time to get splashed.

"Welcome to fatherhood," she laughed as Oliver spit out a mouthful of bubbles.

CHAPTER SEVEN

After his bath, Teresa and Oliver took Thomas outdoors to play for a while. Her, no, *their* son had oodles of energy and needed to expel them in positive ways.

It wasn't easy to be creative with them always living in the city, but here in this lovely forest, though still a bit chilly, Thomas was in heaven. They'd stopped by the water to fish for a little bit. Thomas was still young, but he played and splashed while Ollie did all the work of hooking the fish. He'd caught quite a few after just a little while.

"How did you do that?" She asked eyeing his catch with wonder. He dropped them into the small cooler packed with ice and grinned.

"An old Grizzly secret, I'd tell you, but then I'd have to, you know what," he grinned.

"What if I tickle it out of you? After all I happen to have myself a big, strong Grizzly lover," she said naughtily and loved his growly response.

"Mommy lookee me!" Thomas ran and climbed on some big rocks.

He giggled as Oliver swung him up onto his shoulders. They picked berries and skipped stones on the lake for what seemed like minutes but was really hours. Her heart beat heavily, filled to the brim with emotions she never dared to dream she'd ever feel again. But here she was, and she did, as if those lovely feelings had never gone away or been put on hold.

Love. She gulped audibly. Teresa still loved Oliver Pax. As truly and deeply, and possibly even more than she had two years ago when she'd been a green girl with no knowledge of the very real cruelty that existed in the world.

He hadn't said anything about love, but she was certain she'd felt it in his careful touch. Her eyes rolled back into her head as she thought about the pleasure he'd brought her mere hours ago. The physical side of their relationship had always been explosive.

There was nothing on the planet that could compare to Oliver's lovemaking. Not that she had any experience otherwise. He was her one and only. Surely, he knew that, but if he didn't she could certainly find ways to show him.

Thinking about that made her stomach clench and her needy clit throb with anticipation. Her panties moistened, her breath caught, the need to go to him now, to strip her clothes off and ride him into oblivion coursed through her. Like she was just an empty shell waiting for him to fill her. It was scary, it was heady, hell, she didn't know what to think about this sudden carnal urge to strip them both and indulge in his magnificent body once again.

She coughed to cover up the moan that escaped her lips. Her entire body felt as though it was on fire. Teresa shook with the strength of it. She looked up to find Oliver had stopped chasing Thomas. He stood between the still bare trees, nostrils flaring, his pupils dilated as he watched her like the predator he was.

Eyes bled to black, a great rumbly growl echoed from his chest as he sucked in a great deep breath. The growl grew as he took in her scent. His eyes flashed as he recognized her desire, and damn, but she found it hard to breathe.

He looked so good. Utterly masculine and tempting in his jeans and cotton shirt. Something inside her rumbled in awareness as even more moisture seeped between her thighs. Her sex clenched on air, breasts swelled, and nipples hardened.

Oliver sucked in another deep breath and licked his full lips. That was nearly her undoing. She wanted those lips, craved them on her own, and further down still. She wanted his hands, his mouth on her breasts and belly, and finally, between her thighs.

"Mommy, thirsty!" Thomas ran through the few feet of space that stood between her and Oliver, and she dropped down to capture him in a hug immediately, breaking their strange intense stare.

"Here have some water," she smiled and offered one of the three refillable bottles she'd packed in the small rucksack she'd found in the closet along with some snacks, wipes, tissues, and band-aids for her sweet, but adventurous boy.

Teresa stood and wiped her sweaty hands on her pants before reaching in the bag and offering another bottle to Oliver. He stepped forward crowding her a little, and her heart beat double time.

"Thanks," Oliver winked.

He was still a little breathless after engaging in a game of tickle tag monster with Thomas, or maybe it was from that tempestuous look they'd shared. She couldn't be sure. That gaze had been filled with promises of impending delightful seduction. Maybe if she was lucky, she'd find out just how delightful later.

Their boy gulped down his water greedily and he watched his parents with a twinkle in his bright eyes. The fresh air was good for him. Guilt and shame washed over her as she thought about all the time hiding and on the run. Living in motels and eating ramen noodles out of cheap cartons.

"It's alright now," Oliver said, seeming to read her mind and she offered him a small smile in turn.

"Here, Mommy," Thomas handed her back the water then tucked his hand shyly into Oliver's.

Tears pricked her eyes as she watched the only man who'd ever touched her heart accept the child's hand as if it were the most natural thing in the world. Perhaps it was for Shifters. She wasn't quite sure how the biological dynamic worked in so far as familial relationships between supernaturals.

And yes, there were more things out there than Shifters. Her time in a cell at Witherspoon Tech had shown her that. She shuddered in revulsion, maybe fear, and something inside her rumbled. Teresa stopped moving, her panic rising, threatening to take over.

It was back. That strange sensation of the *other* inside of her. Her body burned and her stomach cramped. Something was scratching at her from the inside out.

A darkness. A demon. What had her father called her? Oh yeah, an evil, cheap, vile bitch. A whore, like her mother, and that she didn't understand at all.

The thing inside her growled at the memory. It's anger obvious, and Teresa almost laughed. At least whatever the darkness was, it seemed to like her at times and it definitely hated her father as much as she did. It pushed again, and her fear increased. She closed her eyes, straining to keep it leashed.

No. She would not give in to darkness now. She pushed that *other thing* deep down inside of her and focused on her two boys. They were her whole heart, she realized quite suddenly. Regret filled her as she saw the hard lines in his face. The untrusting glint that had never been in his eyes before. Damn, she had caused that.

She was responsible for the sorrow lines that creased his brow. But no more. They were together and she would do her best to smooth them all out, if only he'd let her.

Yes, something inside of her spoke.

Teresa ignored that other voice and focused on him. After all this time, she would never love another. Just him. Her Ollie. Like it had always been, but different, better, stronger now for everything they had both experienced.

"Hey, what's wrong?" he said quietly.

"Nothing," she returned, "I just, I feel strange."

"It's okay," he soothed and went to touch her shoulder, but stopped suddenly.

The sound of twigs snapping had all three heads turning to look. Oliver moved in front of both her and Thomas, shielding them with his big body. Teresa felt every muscle inside of her clench and strain. Prepared for something, though she hardly knew what. The need to protect her son was paramount in that moment.

It only let up the moment Oliver relaxed his own stance. Trusting him implicitly, she waited for him to explain. Of course, patience was never one of her virtues. Curiosity got the better of her, so she peeked around him.

It was a woman, she soon realized. A lovely woman.

And, much to Teresa's rising anger, she was not a stranger to Oliver. She watched as he smiled warmly at the stranger with her long straight hair. Locks that Teresa had always envied for her own unruly waves were certainly a bitch to tame at times.

The stranger had big amber eyes behind rather stylish glasses, and they too, smiled up at her Ollie behind thick lashes. She was tall and lean, more slender than Teresa at any rate, but it was her easy grace and confidence that she belonged there, *with him*, that stuck in her craw.

Jealousy surged, irrational and misplaced, maybe, but she couldn't help it. In fact, she seemed to not be fully in control of her emotions at all.

"Mommy? You're rumbly like my *grisle!*" Thomas said.

She looked at her cub and panic had her hyperventilating. A deep, gnawing rumble started in her chest, and Oliver whipped his head around to catch her in his curious stare. He lifted Thomas out of her arms when she thrust him towards his father.

"Thomas," she said the boy's name and dropped down.

Her body tensed, a flash of pain shot through her stomach, like a cramp, but much more direct and acute. The pain seemed to grow as quickly as it had come on, but she hardly noticed it in the face of the raw jealousy that had threatened to consume her.

Teresa was scared for her son, but something inside of her told her she would never harm the child. No, not the child, *their child*, their *cub*. Whatever was happening, it was happening now. Every inch of her burned with hurt.

"Resa?" Oliver's eyes went wide.

He motioned for Thomas to move behind him, which thankfully the cub did.

"I'll take him," the strange woman said, and that really pissed off the thing inside Teresa.

She snarled and snapped at her. Burning, itching, gnawing pain shot through every cell inside of her. She felt as if she were being torn into pieces. Loud snapping, tearing, cracking noises echoed in her ears along with the sound of her blood thundering in her ears.

"It's okay, Thomas, go sit by Jennifer," he said and Teresa snapped her jaws around teeth that weren't hers, "Teresa? Look at me, don't fight it, baby, it's okay," Oliver dropped to his knees in front of her.

Poor man. He looked as though he were the one in pain, being torn apart but it was her. She was being eaten, consumed, ravaged by whatever monstrous demon her father had injected her with.

"Thomas," she growled around her misshaped mouth, worried for the safety of her son despite the thing's insistence he was safe.

"He's fine. I'm worried about you, love. Listen to me, you have to stop fighting. Trust me, it is not what you think," he said, and she saw the Bear bleed into his eyes.

That beautiful, strong, dominant Grizzly of his was staring at her. Suddenly, Teresa stilled and quieted. She did as he asked and stopped fighting. Then, the most marvelous thing happened.

Mate, she heard a voice inside her head.

Her whole body though wracked with pain, seemed to heed that distant whisper. It was as if the sound was reaching for her through some sort of thick, hazy fog.

She turned to Oliver for help, only he didn't look like himself. His facial features contorted under her watchful gaze as more of his Bear leaked through. Something inside of her responded to it almost violently. No, not violence. A rapid succession of emotions filtered through to her. The most urgent were need, desire, and most of all *love*, she realized.

Mate, the voice repeated more clear than last time.

It wasn't scary this time. It felt right. Teresa relaxed her body and embraced the fire inside. In doing so, she felt as if her skin was being touched and stroked by the softest of hands. An electric hum seemed to fill her ears and the fire grew in intensity for the briefest of moments.

Magic, the voice whispered, *let me in*.

Teresa felt as though she were being ripped in two. She had only one choice and she chose to trust in Oliver. She acknowledged the power flowing through her and prayed to God and whoever else was listening to keep the ones she loved safe during whatever was happening to her.

"That's it, Resa, let her in," Oliver coaxed and she heard the wonder in his voice and relished the scent of faith and love that all seemed to come from him.

Finally, she willed herself to relax. She closed her eyes and groaned, commanding the muscles in her body to unclench and loosen. Only it wasn't her body. Not her usual one anyway.

Teresa stood on shaky, powerful, fur-covered legs, four of them to be exact. What the ever-loving hell just happened to her?

A roar erupted from her mouth, and she opened her eyes to see that the world looked different to her somehow, it was sharper more acute. She blinked rapidly to see Oliver standing in front of her with his arms wide as he directed her focus to him.

"Look at me, look at me, Resa," he commanded and she did, reluctantly.

She did not want to obey her mate. She wanted to run, to play, to hunt, maybe even fish. Oh yes, Bears loved to fish!

Bears? Me? A Bear?

Rawr! Her answer flowed from her maw and Teresa fell backwards onto her big furry butt.

"You're so beautiful, baby," Oliver grinned wickedly and took a cautious step forward,

Damn right he should be careful. She was a Bear! Not just any bear, but a full grown Grizzly Sow!

"You're a Shifter," he said once more with awe in his voice.

"Mommy's a *grisle*," Thomas said.

Teresa turned to see the strange woman holding her son and she saw red.

Grrr.

CHAPTER EIGHT

Teresa chuffed and snorted angrily. She pawed the ground, but Oliver stepped between her and the stranger who dared touch her cub.

"Easy, baby, she's a friend."

Easy? Oh no, he didn't. She tried to yell at him to tell him she wanted that slut away from her baby. A few other choice curses filled her head, but she couldn't talk. She tried again and heard more growling and snarling.

"Don't panic, use your mind not your mouth to speak to me," he instructed.

Oliver! She screamed his name in panic inside her mind's eye.

"I hear you, baby," he answered and shook his ear.

Oops. So, she yelled a little bit too loudly. But she needed answers. She dropped to all fours and stomped her feet.

"Easy, love," he approached cautiously, "may I?"

Hands raised in her direction, Teresa nodded at him.

Mate, that inner voice chuffed happily and Teresa

found herself rumbling pleasantly as Oliver stroked his big, strong hands through her fur.

Fur?

Yes, answered the voice, *we have magnificent fur.*

"Sweet mate, you do have a lovely coat," he said and brought his forehead to hers.

"You've been cooped up a long time, haven't you?"

A deep, mournful growl sounded from her Bear's lips and Teresa felt shame fill her. But how could she have known? Her mother had died in childbirth and her father was a *normal.*

Not our father, her she-Bear growled.

Suddenly, she knew the truth. Teresa was not the daughter of Mathias Witherspoon. He didn't have the right scent. But why had he claimed she was his daughter?

"We will find the answers, love, but for now, want to run with me?"

Her Bear's happy rumble cut short when she snorted in the direction of their cub.

"We won't go far. Jennifer is a friend. I swear to you. She would never harm our son. Jennifer?"

"We will walk back to your cabin and wait there for you, alright?" the woman, no, the Owl Shifter, said, and Teresa watched her go with a warning growl.

"Come on," Oliver removed his clothing and within seconds he stood before her a magnificent Grizzly Bear, much larger than her own.

Together they ran through the woods, over the budding shrubs and patches of snow, down to the rocky shore on that side of the lake just behind the cabin. She took a moment to admire her handsome Grizzly before he shimmered back to a man before her eyes.

"Will you change back now, beautiful? Let me have my, mate," he told her.

Wow. Teresa caught sight of her reflection in the water. She had fur, and claws, and huge teeth.

Gulp. Okay. She could live with that. But that wasn't what had her reluctant to change back. No, it was the fact that he had just called her mate. That word alone meant everything to her.

"That's it, sweet, your cub and your mate need you to change back," Oliver cajoled.

Be with our mate now, her Bear suggested and she closed her eyes and willed her human body forward.

"Wow," she said as Oliver waited a beat before putting his arms around her.

They stood in three feet of freezing lake water, and suddenly she felt a tad conspicuous out in the open with nothing at all covering her body.

"You're lovely, Resa," he said and claimed her mouth in a searching kiss that she was desperate to explore.

After some time, however long, she was unsure, Teresa opened her eyes. Oliver had lifted her shivering body out of the cold water and held her against his warmth while plundering her mouth. Her inner Sow reveled in his possession. Patches of snow still littered the rocky shore so he carried her to a large tree and used it for leverage while covering the bark with his hands.

"Need you," he grunted, but waited for her hands to travel between them.

She gripped his heavy cock in her hands and placed him at her slick entrance. The tree was rough under her bare ass, but she did not care. All she wanted was him.

"That's actually kind of funny," Oliver said as he allowed just the tip of his dick to pierce her slick heat.

"Why funny?" She asked.

"Because love, a moment ago you actually had a Bear ass," he grinned and instead of fear or disgust she saw utter joy in his gaze.

"Please," she rolled her eyes and begged him, ignoring her accidental pun.

She needed him now, desperately, and she wasn't too proud to show him just how much. Her body throbbed and ached in places she'd neglected for far too long it would seem. Being with him again sparked her senses, ignited her heart, and fanned the flame of desire she'd thought extinguished.

Mine, her Bear whispered inside her mind and she welcomed the thought.

"Mate," he grunted as if in response and all traces of humor fled his gaze.

Oliver needed no more coaxing after that. She clung to his shoulders as he made love to her beneath the setting sun. The cold went unnoticed as her magnificently muscled mate moved fiercely, passionately over her, giving her pleasure that only he could deliver.

Oliver mashed his lips to hers. He didn't stop kissing her, not even when stars exploded behind her eyes and the whole world spiraled out of focus.

"Ollie," she gasped his name, trying to catch her breath as tiny little aftershocks continued to tremble between them from the place where his body still possessed hers all the way to that muscle that was pounding furiously inside her chest.

When they were both finally sated, Oliver kissed her gently. He carried her princess style up the steps he must've had carved into the stone, leading to his back porch.

"I'm too heavy," she started.

"You're light as a feather," he snorted.

"They'll see us," she sat up when she heard Thomas inside the cabin giggling brightly.

"No worries, love, you go shower and I'll bring up a tray."

A while later, Teresa wandered back downstairs to where Oliver was chatting with Jennifer while he prepared dinner.

"Hi," his eyes found her and she smiled at him a little shy since she her new senses told her this woman was a Shifter and she would know what they had been up to in the woods just behind the cabin.

"Well, I think proper introductions are in order," the stranger said brightly.

Teresa's eyes snapped to the woman's oval shaped face. It was strange now, but she felt her Bear deep within her assessing the situation. The animal inside of her might've been in a rage of jealousy earlier, or maybe her Bear saw this person as some sort of proprietorial challenger, but not now. Now, she was the woman who had taken care of Teresa's cub and for that she was grateful.

"Thomas? Why don't you come over here and let your mom see you're alright," the stranger spoke up.

It was a good idea. Yes. Teresa wanted her cub. She scooped up her son and felt Thomas cling to her. Immediately, the animal within stopped her grumbling. Scaring her cub was not on her list of things to do that day.

"Mommy," Thomas squealed when he ran to her, pumping his chubby little legs as he did.

He'd been playing on a plush throw rug in the center of the large living room that was visible from where she stood. She could make out the box of crayons he'd upended everywhere, a few coloring books, his new cars, and a few of the dolls he had brought with him. The place was a mess, but the good kind, she thought fondly.

"Hello, my sweet boy," she dropped a dozen quick kiss on his forehead, nose, and cheeks all while cuddling him close.

Thomas liked it when she did that and he laughed out loud. He smelled like forest and sunshine, and yes, just beneath that, a hint of fur. Her little whirlwind squirmed after a moment or two, and she released him. He was a happy and healthy cub, anxious to get back to his toys.

"So, Teresa," a voice interrupted her musings and she turned back to the two adults, "I'm Jennifer."

"Hello," she answered.

Oliver walked over to her wiping his hands on a dish towel before he reached for her, tugging her close to his big, hard body. She loved the sheer size and strength of him, leaning into his touch she inhaled his scent and savored it before releasing her breath.

He brushed her lips with a soft hello kiss and pressed his forehead to hers with one hand on the back of her neck. The touch was welcomed, cherished in fact by woman and Sow. It was quite something for her to admit these things, to feel them so fully now that she had embraced her true self.

"You okay?" he asked.

"Yeah, I'm adjusting quickly actually, but I guess I'm sort of confused."

"I can only imagine," his concern shone through his dark eyes as he brushed a curl behind her ear, "What did that bastard father of yours do to you?" He growled.

"Yes, I'd be curious as well," Jennifer interrupted from her perch on one of the sturdy chairs in the dining room.

Teresa's eyes flicked to the woman, but before she could respond Thomas ran straight to *Jennifer* from the living room. She watched in shock as he climbed on the woman's lap and whispered something in her ear. Jennifer laughed brightly before letting him down again. Teresa watched the harmless byplay, but she was unable to fully control the growl that built up inside her.

"Easy, she-Bear, I have not harmed your cub," Jennifer said and nodded in Thomas' direction, "he is safe and well, see?"

"I swear to you, Teresa," Oliver interjected, "I wouldn't have left him with her if I didn't trust her. She's a friend."

That only made the growl grow that much louder. Uh oh. She shook her head to try and regain some control.

"Well, this the whole family then?" Jennifer nodded in Teresa's direction and she found herself smiling at the other woman.

Okay, it was more snarl than smile, and Teresa immediately stilled. What the hell was wrong with her?

"I see," Jennifer laughed, "well, would it help you to know that I am not interested in Oliver that way," she cocked her head and stared at Teresa with piercing predatory eyes before warming them.

Her birdlike gaze darted to young Thomas, who was watching them with a concerned expression on his cherubic face.

"Maybe we can be properly introduced now that Mommy isn't going to fight her Bear anymore?"

"Mommy's grisle!" Thomas said from the other room.

"Yes, Thomas that's right Mommy's a Grizzly, just like your Daddy, and you. Teresa, allow me to welcome you officially to the world of Shifters," Jennifer gave a little bow.

CHAPTER NINE

Teresa might have been under the influence of a certain green-eyed monster a few hours ago, but looking at the warm smile on Jennifer's face, she and her Bear came to a decision. If Oliver trusted this woman, then so would she.

"Why don't we all sit and have a chat?" she suggested.

Thomas was still in sight, and she supposed she needed some answers too. Being a Bear was new, so was being with Oliver again. Still, she didn't fuss when her Grizzly lover tugged her onto his lap.

He was a very physical person, always wanting to touch her, hold her. She remembered that from before, and to be truthful, it was one of the things she'd loved best.

Her father, no, that was wrong, *Mathias Witherspoon* was not the hugging kind. She'd had little in the way of hugs and kisses growing up. That came with being raised by nannies and attending private schools her whole life. She was practically starved for any little crumb of physical affection by the time she'd met Ollie, and he'd given her so much more than that.

His head was cocked to the side and she saw his intelligent brown eyes searching hers for answers. Unfortunately, she didn't have any for either of them.

"First, I want you to know Teresa that I've known Jennifer for a long time. She is just a friend. There is no reason for you to be jealous of her or anyone, I swear," he told her.

"I'm sorry, I don't know what came over me," she said.

It was the truth. She didn't know exactly why she'd had such a strong reaction only that she was a Bear now. Or, she always had been, but now she was finally in contact with her animal side. Perhaps there was something about the nature of Shifters that made them jealous of their significant others? The fact that he seemed amused under his worry made her feel slightly foolish.

"No, I don't mean to tease," he said, reading her mind again, "it's just you remind me of me."

"How so?"

"Hell, Resa, don't you remember how I used to get those rare times we left my apartment and went to eat or wander through the park?"

"Yeah," she laughed at the memory, "you always got so growly, but I thought that was because of your Bear."

"It was. It is. A dominant Shifter like me wants to keep his mate to himself, especially since at the time you were unmarked."

"Mate? Unmarked?"

"Shit, I suppose I should explain."

"That might be good," Jennifer said amusedly, but Teresa was too focused on Oliver to pay attention to the woman.

"Remember that last night," he started and memories began to flood her mind, of course she remembered it. So much pleasure followed by the most intense heartbreak of her young life.

"I mean specifically, the sex.," he said without embarrassment, though she felt her cheeks burn.

"Ollie," she whispered.

"Sex is very natural, Teresa, I assure you I know all about the birds and the bees," the woman grinned at her remark.

"Sorry, love, I have no wish to embarrass you," he reassured her.

"I know. To answer, yes, I remember," she whispered back trying to wrap her head around everything that had just happened.

"So, when I shifted were you expecting that?"

"No, love. But I am happy you did. You are the most beautiful she-Bear I have ever seen."

Something inside of her, *her Bear* she supposed, chuffed happily at his praise. Okay. So her Bear was a slut for a compliment. At that thought, the Bear snarled, and Teresa shushed the beast. She was entitled to a little freak out wasn't she?

Sheesh!

"Anyway, I bit you that night. Do you remember?" he added.

She nodded her head. Of course, she recalled the passionate love bite he'd given her. In his enthusiasm, he'd broken skin, and left a small scar just below her left ear. She still had that scar. Had traced it over and over again during their years apart, whenever missing him had seemed almost impossibly painful. It gave her peace and she'd felt connected to him whenever she touched it.

"That wasn't an ordinary bite, Resa. I never got to explain it then, but please, allow me to now."

"Alright," she waited and Oliver lifted her hair over her shoulder and found the scar with his fingertips.

She shivered at the slight brush of his hands and more so when his lips touched it in a small, simple kiss.

"This is my mating mark, Teresa," he looked at her with glittering black eyes.

She knew it was his Bear pressing forward, and she felt no fear. Only wonder and love. In fact, the beast residing inside of her rose to meet that gaze. Ollie blinked and growled in his throat. A possessive comforting sound, she somehow understood.

"You see, a mating mark is a bite from a Shifter to his fated mate signaling to all and the universe itself that they belong together. This bite means you are mine, sweet. Claimed by me, for eternity."

Teresa swallowed and almost slipped off his lap. She would have if he hadn't been holding her so securely. She tried to comprehend what he was saying. His fated mate.

Could it be true? She'd heard some stories in her wanderings, but that would mean that he loved her. Could he? Even after what she'd done to him.

"Ollie?" she glanced at Thomas, their son was happily playing away.

"Resa?"

Teresa refocused on Oliver. She had so many questions, so many stimuli hitting her at once. She raised her hands to his shoulders to steady herself. The world seemed off its axis. Everything was askew, except for him. Ollie was just so big and strong, so constant, and dependable. Like an oak. God, she loved him.

"DO you understand what I am saying? You're it for me, Teresa. My one and only. When you left, I thought I would die, but you're back now. I swear to do everything I can to keep you and Thomas safe, just say you will stay. Please."

"You're saying you still l-love me?" tears pricked her eyes.

"Always, mate," his arms contracted around her, "I love you, want you, need you, more with each passing minute. You are my fated mate. There is nothing on this earth or any other more important to me."

"Oh, Oliver," she wrapped him tightly in her arms, heart soaring at his words, "I love you too."

His chest rumbled pleasantly, and she recognized it as his Grizzly Bear. Her own Sow rose up inside of her, and for the first time she saw in her mind's eye the complete image of her Grizzly Bear.

"Oh my God. I can't believe I'm a Shifter!"

CHAPTER TEN

Oliver smiled at Thomas while he cut up vegetables for lunch. After last night's discussion, Jennifer had gone home with the promise to return today for a longer chat. That gave him the night with his family.

Thomas was such a sweet cub. He was so proud of Teresa for the incredible job she'd done bearing and raising him under impossible circumstances. Of course, he was angry he could not be there for them then, but he would be now.

They'd spent the rest of the night in each other's arms, talking about the long years apart. He understood she'd been afraid of Mathias and Witherspoon Tech, and even worse, she'd been made to feel scared of her own Bear.

The very thought enraged his beast. No Shifter should ever be forced apart from his or her own animal. It was blasphemy! He wanted to hunt down the bastards who'd drugged and experimented on her and tear them to shreds. It was his right as her mate.

Already, he'd set the wheels rolling and had alerted the

proper Shifter agencies, including the High Council. If Witherspoon wasn't on their watchlist before, the bastard was now.

The wind whipped through the open window and he looked to see more flurries falling from the skies. Spring was late in coming, but he didn't mind it. Not when he had a mate and cub to snuggle with. Thomas liked the fireplace last night, a little too much and he'd quickly made a mental note to babyproof the cabin and his other homes.

They hadn't really discussed the future, but there was no way he was letting either of them go. Not now. Not ever. Still, they had some things to discuss, one thing Oliver understood now was the importance of total honesty with his mate.

For that, they needed to finish talking about her so-called father. Then he could tell her what plans were being made to protect both her and their cub.

Cooking gave him time to gather his thoughts and as he prepped the side dishes, Jennifer sat sipping tea with Teresa at the table. From what he could gather, the two women were getting along, which was an immense relief to him.

The idea that Teresa thought him capable of wanting another made his Bear snarl and stomp inside of him. The animal wanted to console her, to take her over his shoulder, bring her upstairs, and fuck her until she understood he wanted no one else.

Of course, that kind of thing would have to wait until they were back home in a soundproofed room. He already had people working on that. Oh, he would still make love to her while they were here.

He wanted her to know how much he loved and adored her in every single way possible. Then maybe he could broach the subject of claiming her once more with her full consent and knowledge.

Once little Thomas had gone to sleep, Oliver had made sure Teresa had an idea of just how much he wanted her. Three times last night alone. He just couldn't help himself, and why should he try? Fuck proprieties and all the rest. She was his mate. The mother of his cub.

He grinned as he thought of his sweet boy. His cub was smart and funny, a fast learner too. In one afternoon, he'd taught him how to pick the sweetest berries and recite the names of almost all the trees around them. He even watched the tyke get six skips across the lake with a small stone.

He was a proud papa. Couldn't wait to show him off to Terence, Chance, and the others. Over the years, Oliver had become friends with a small, tight group of supernaturals and their mates. One of those couples had recently had a child. Maybe Avail's babe could prove a good playmate for his own cub. The Leeds Mansion was quite the estate and the new father was already readying the grounds for a custom playground that could withstand anything his Devilish offspring could throw at it.

Hmm. That was something to think about too. Oliver had a great apartment in the city, but surely his family would prefer a real house. A home in the suburbs maybe, or down by the ocean with a nice forest backdrop. Maccon City was well-known amongst supernaturals as a great place to raise a family. *A safe place,* which was the most important thing to him.

"Daddy! Want nummies," Thomas ran into his knees, and Oliver was shocked by the fact he'd almost been toppled by a toddler.

The cub was stronger than even the average Shifter,

and he'd been off balance trying to reach a baking dish he'd put on the top cabinet for some foolish reason or other.

"Easy, buddy," he said, and handed the cub a carrot, "here snack on this until it's ready."

"Nummies!"

"Yes, nummies, next I am grilling some of that fish we caught in the lake yesterday. Like fish?" he teased the cub.

"Fishies," he giggled.

"That's right, Daddy's making fishies, with extra butter and lemon on top," he winked as the tyke scampered off back to the living room where he'd been systematically marking his territory with toys. Little cutie.

Oliver frowned as he shook the box of rice. It had only been a couple of days, and already they were halfway through his food supply. He'd have to go back in a day or so. His sensitive ears picked up bits of conversation coming from the women and his heart squeezed in his chest as he heard Teresa recite some of the horrors of her past. He looked down to see he'd crushed the stainless-steel serving spoon in his hand at her words.

"My father, no I guess I can't call him that anymore. Okay, so Witherspoon Tech had me locked in a cell for about three months, but in that short time they ran all sorts of tests. They took my blood, monitored my heart, my sleep, and they gave me injections. I think they drugged my food too. The man I thought was my father had always been crazy strict about my diet most of my life. He'd insisted on a solid vitamin regime too. I took pills blindly from the time I hit puberty until I ran away."

"I see," Jennifer said, "did those vitamins come in a bottle?"

"Oh no, just a plastic cup. They were already separated

for me, but I always hated taking them I just never fought him."

"Did you ever stop taking them that is?" Jennifer asked.

"Yeah, actually, for those months when I was with Oliver. I went off the vitamins or whatever they were because they made me feel sick all the time," she shrugged, "In fact, that was why I spent so much time in the park to begin with. That was where we met. The sunlight and fresh air made me feel better."

"Teresa, did you ever see anything with an inscription on it like a bug or beetle at Witherspoon Tech?"

"Yes, I did. Oliver?" she called him, and he went to her side immediately, "Remember when I told you about the beetle?"

"Yes," he nodded and looked at Jennifer, "she mentioned this the first night after the hospital."

Jennifer leaned forward and pursed her lips. Oliver knew the Owl Shifter had a past she didn't like to speak of, but he sometimes wondered about it. There were many hidden organizations in the Shifter world, many societies and councils tasked with one important job, to keep their secret. He knew Jennifer had once worked for one of them.

"I can hear your mind whirring, Oliver Pax, and no, I can't answer your questions. Suffice it to say the group I suspect of being involved in your mate's abduction and imprisonment uses the scarab as a signature of sorts. They have been on our radar for an awfully long time, but we did not know Witherspoon Tech was involved. This information is extremely useful."

"There were others," Teresa said, and looked at him first, then at Jennifer with tears pricking her jade eyes, "others in cells. I couldn't help them. Once I found out I was pregnant, I ran. He said he'd kill you, Oliver, he would hunt you down like an animal, and I couldn't risk it, not then. I had to keep you safe and Thomas too. Then when I thought, that is, when I suspected that whatever they had injected me with was taking over, I came to you for help. I didn't know it was my Bear, and I'm glad I didn't, because it brought me back to you," she sniffed and wiped her face.

"I know, love, I would never want you hurt, but I am so glad you are here now," he kissed her on her head and pulled her close, "but I'm, glad you know your Bear isn't evil. She is part of you, always was and that bastard did something to her. Trust your Bear's instincts to protect you and Thomas both. They don't use the term mama bear lightly you know."

"I've been running for so long. I only just came back to New York after seeing one of Witherspoon Tech's henchmen in Pennsylvania."

"You were that close?"

"Yeah. I couldn't stand being so far as it was. I tried California once, but it made me physically sick, I didn't understand it then."

"That was a result of you stretching your tentative *matebond*," Jennifer supplied, "Oliver marked you, and being away from him would've caused significant physical distress. Shifters are not built to be separated from their one and true mates for very long or for great distances. I imagine you are right and those so-called vitamins were Shifter gene suppressors of some sort."

"So, how is it that I am a Shifter?" she turned in his arms and looked at Jennifer.

"I imagine your natural parents, one or both were Shifters. Perhaps even a grandparent. It has been known to skip a generation. Whatever he did to you, it doesn't seem to have done permanent damage. Your she-Bear was strong yesterday when I saw her. Also, I suspect it is why your son's Bear is showing signs early."

"What do you mean?" Oliver injected.

He felt Teresa's rising fear as if it were his own. Maybe it was. Parenthood did strange things to a man.

"Is Thomas okay?" she asked.

"Yes, he is fine," Jennifer laughed, "though I suspect he will experience his first shift sooner rather than later. It won't hurt him, his Bear couldn't. It is just exceedingly rare for one so young, but with you as his parents I believe Thomas will adjust beautifully."

"Thank you. I sensed his Bear was remarkably close to the surface when I first saw him," Oliver admitted.

He rubbed his hands up and down his mate's spine to soothe her agitation and worry.

"But he will be fine?" his mate asked again looking for reassurance.

"Like I said, it is rare for a cub to shift so early, but there is really no such thing as normal in the supernatural world. When you live as long as I have, you've pretty much seen it all," Jennifer lifted her tea and sipped.

"Thank you, it means a lot to have my questions answered," Teresa sagged against him.

"Just how old are you, Jennifer?" Oliver grinned to lighten the mood.

"And you know better than that," she glared.

"Ollie! Never ask a lady how old she is," Teresa laughed and pinched him on the stomach.

"Ouch!" he laughed, his mood lightening with her own contagious happiness.

The woman was truly a wonder. An idea sprang into his head just then. He kissed her nose and turned to the mysterious Owl Shifter.

"Stay for supper, Jennifer?"

"Yes, please do!" Teresa seconded.

"Jenny!" his cub yelled and came running, "color me!"

"Okay, sweet cub, we can color," Jennifer smiled at Thomas then nodded at Oliver.

With the cub occupied, Oliver and Teresa worked side by side prepping the rest of the meal, but he nudged her away when it came time to set the table and carry the dishes out. It was his privilege to serve dinner to his family and friend on the patio. They laughed and ate the delicious fish with herbed rice and veggies that they had prepared. It all tasted better to him somehow, richer, and sweeter. Oliver insisted on cleaning the dishes and put everything away.

"You'll make her a handy mate," Jennifer walked into the kitchen and placed her cup on the counter.

Darn woman always knew when he was brooding. He supposed he should just give in and tell her already.

"You know, I got the supplies you asked for. I forgot to give them to you. They are in the hall closet, but I was wondering if you wouldn't mind staying and babysitting for us?"

"Oh, big plans?"

"Look, my mate just found out what she is. I think maybe she needs some comforting. It's a big change for her," he shrugged.

"And you want to reaffirm your mating. Ugh, just please don't stay within range of my hearing Bear, or I swear you will never see another jar of my boysenberry jam!"

"I swear," he grinned.

Was he blushing? Shit. He shook his head and filled the kettle.

"Where is Teresa?"

"She's giving Thomas his bath. He slid on a bit of snow

right into a muddy pile of leaves after you brought the dishes inside. The little scamp," she laughed.

Her amber eyes glowed with her Owl and Oliver stopped what he was doing. He understood the animal inside her was sizing him up.

"You will do fine by her, Oliver, don't worry. I'll watch your cub."

"Thank you, Jennifer."

"Thomas is in his room," Teresa walked into the kitchen and straight by his side.

He loved that part of her that recognized that he was where she belonged. So much so, he took advantage of it, wrapping her in his arms and nuzzling her neck. Her peaches and cream scent filled his nostrils and he felt his pulse race just being near her.

"He's asking for you Jennifer, would you mind?"

It amazed him how quickly she'd changed her opinion on Jennifer. Some of it was his word that he trusted the Owl Shifter, the rest, he suspected, was her own Bear giving the woman the thumbs up.

"Actually, I was just telling Oliver he should take you for a little twilight stroll while I mind the cub," Jennifer smiled.

The blasted woman stole his idea! Oliver rolled his eyes at her then squeezed his mate. She was looking at him curiously.

"Want to go for a walk with me, love?" he asked.

"Sure, but you don't mind Jennifer?" Teresa asked.

"It would be my pleasure."

"Great. Thank you," Oliver said to Jennifer, then turned to his sweetly blushing mate, "give me a sec, love, then we can go."

CHAPTER ELEVEN

Teresa spent the last day and a half marveling at the fact that she was not a monster. That the man she thought was her father had not injected her with some sort of demon like she'd suspected. She was in fact, a Shifter.

"Actually," Oliver interrupted her thoughts, "demons are like Shifters too. A friend of mine, my producer, you met him at the hospital in fact. Anyway, Chance is the son of a luck Demon."

"Did you just read my mind?" she asked in surprise.

"Uh, no love, you were talking out loud," he looked at her strangely, and she closed her eyes in embarrassment.

That was a quirk of hers from years ago, thinking out loud. She'd only ever done it when she was with him. Would she ever not act the fool around this man?

Sigh.

"You're not a fool, and you speak your mind because you know you can trust me. It's an honor, sweet, one that I cherish," he squeezed her hand as they neared the path that led to the cabin.

With Thomas back at the cabin safe and secure with the state of the art system Oliver had installed and with Jennifer with him, Teresa could relax and just enjoy being with him. Jennifer was actually quite nice, Teresa admitted reluctantly.

"Yeah," Oliver agreed, "you got to know each other a little, right?" he asked.

"Yes. She is nice and I feel like we can trust her," she said and allowed her Bear to rise up a bit to measure the truth in her words.

There was no doubt, only trust. Good, she sighed with relief. She had the oddest sensation of completion whenever she allowed her, she-Bear to come out even just a little.

That is because we are one, two sides of one person, the voice she'd feared for so long spoke inside of her mind, and instead of being scared, Teresa felt only joy.

"I know, it can be overwhelming meeting your animal spirit for the first time," Jennifer had said kindly earlier that afternoon. She'd handed Teresa a mug of herbal tea and a napkin.

Hell, Teresa hadn't even been aware that she'd been crying. She blotted her cheeks and eyes and smiled at the woman whom she now thought of as a friend. The Sow inside of her grumbled gently and she knew she did right in trusting Jennifer. The following snort was one she recognized as her Bear expressing happiness.

"Shall we chat? Get to know each other and your circumstances a bit?" Jennifer had offered over tea, "you know I have only ever been a friend to Oliver. He's gotten quite the reputation as a grumpy old Bear in your absence," the woman laughed.

"Now, don't growl," Jennifer mock scolded and Teresa cut off the sound.

"Sorry," she said, "this is all so new, and yet it feels perfect. Like I have been missing something my whole life, some piece of myself, and I guess that make sense, because I have."

"Yes, and now you have your Bear, your cub, and your mate in one place. She is going to push you to mark him, you know."

"Yes, my, uh, hormones seem to already be a little out of control when it comes to my Ollie," she felt her cheeks burn with embarrassment at her familiar use of the nickname she'd called him years ago.

"Ollie, huh? Well, don't be shy now, dear. We are, all of us here, dual-natured spirits with primordial instincts, supernatural powers, and real actual animals living inside of us. Mating is serious business, and an unclaimed fated mate is fiercely coveted by his or her significant other or others."

"Others?"

"Why, yes, some Shifters have multiple partners in a mating. It is accepted as tradition and sometimes expected in Packs or Clans where a Triad rules."

"Really?" she'd giggled at the scandalous thought, but then her Bear assured her it was quite natural.

"Oh my, you are positively delightful, the Fates and Oliver have chosen well for him. You will be good together," Jennifer, the wise Owl Shifter and Teresa's newest friend, had stated matter-of-factly.

"Thanks, let's just hope Ollie means it when he says he wants me for keeps. I don't think I can let him go now," she said and felt the truth in her words in her Bear's grumbling response.

"You definitely don't need to worry about that," Jennifer reassured her.

The two had talked some more while Oliver finished

preparing supper. He was handy in the kitchen she noted with glee as cooking was one of her most hated chores. She'd rather fold towels to be honest. Plus, he was good at it. The food was absolutely delicious. She never realized she loved fish so much.

"Bears like fish," he smiled and winked at her which led her to believe she'd blurted some of her thoughts while they'd been walking along the woods aloud.

"Only a few, love," he answered, "about the food though, my rather superior grilling skills aside, Bears do like a good fish."

"Yes well, Thomas certainly had," she giggled.

"Yes," Oliver smiled, "I love him, you know. Something inside of me just lights up when I see him."

"I can tell," she said and meant it.

There was something about the usually serious and dignified Oliver Pax crawling around on all fours making silly faces at his barely two-year-old cub, that simply melted her heart. She enjoyed watching them as they chased each other and played together, getting to know one another over the past few days.

"You know Jennifer teased me about you being a keeper and all since you cook and clean too."

"Oh yeah?"

"You're not bad looking either," Teresa shrugged.

"Is that so?" he snorted and she kept her face even while she pretended to look him up and down with a critical eye.

"You'll do," she bit back her grin.

"I see," Oliver straightened to his full height and faced her.

Love swelled inside of her until she thought she would burst with it, but she kept her expression simple, except for the twitch at the corner of her mouth. The man was quick to spot it and he gave her a smoldering look that made her want to jump his bones.

Everything she had ever wanted her whole life was finally within her grasp. She just had to take it. Was she brave enough to grab onto happiness with both hands and never let go?

Teresa inhaled deeply, biting back tears. It was as if all her emotions were simply too much for her, they threatened to spill over and bubble out like those same tears that pricked her eyes.

She thought about the past two years and leaving Oliver. It had been the most difficult thing she'd ever had to do. Running to protect their son was a no brainer. Thank God it was all over now and the hard life she and Thomas had been living, was truly behind them now. Thomas would have a real home with parents who loved him.

Mate, her Bear pushed the thought at her and this time, she readily welcomed it.

Thomas had already accepted Oliver with that wonderful perseverance, flexibility, and endurance all children had and adults could only dream of. Before they'd left, she'd kissed his head and said she'd loved him to which he'd answered back that he loved Mommy *and* Daddy.

She'd seen the way the matter of fact statement had touched Oliver. The big Grizzly had nearly teared up. She could still hear the echoes of Thomas' laughter and the car sounds he made while racing the red toy car against the blue one, his parents temporarily forgotten as he played with Jennifer. It had made both of them smile all the way down the lane and into the woods.

Their cub was a good boy. He deserved this chance to have a real family. She'd moved him around so much in his young life. She had no idea how good it would feel to be back here for the both of them. To be home with Oliver. Her mate and Thomas' father.

She cursed her own stupidity for believing her lying, scheming, violent pretend father. The idea that Witherspoon Tech was out there and still searching for her scared the crap out of Teresa. But, and it was a big but, she finally understood why Mathias Witherspoon wanted to keep her away from the man she loved. Pure and simple malice.

He wanted to keep you from your true inner strength. To keep you apart from me. I am your strength, I am the other half to your soul. We are one, her Bear spoke to her, supplying answers to questions she hadn't even asked. Rage like she never felt before towards her parent filled her hard and fast.

Grrr.

Teresa closed her eyes and pushed the beast back down. She didn't want to be filled with hate. Not now, not ever. Thomas deserved better than that from her, so did Oliver.

Mate. Claim. Mine, her Bear chuffed.

She opened her eyes and walked alongside her mate. Perhaps with a little luck and some patience, she would find out what being mates really meant for them both. She had no doubts in her mind that together they would be stronger, better, happier than she'd ever been alone.

Together, they would be a family.

Yes, agreed her Bear, *good plan.*

CHAPTER TWELVE

Using the rucksack Teresa had found in the back of his closet the day before, Oliver had stuffed an oversized throw blanket inside, a couple of stainless-steel tumblers, and a vintage bottle of red wine he'd been saving for a special occasion.

He had thought to celebrate the finished version of *Where Beauty Lives* alone with this bottle, but this was so much better. It might not be the most planned out evening, but it would be perfect.

Mate, Oliver's Bear grumbled inside of him, anxious and impatient to get started. If all went well, he would reclaim his sweet Teresa under the stars this very night. Nerves danced along his spine and butterflies turned into fighter jets inside his stomach.

He was as nervous as a green cub. His Bear chuffed and snorted, laughing at his human side. Then he got serious, the Grizzly inside of him demanded that he do everything in his power to not fuck this up.

Oliver was full on board with that plan. Teresa was his now and forever. He just needed to prove to them both that he was a worthy mate, his beast a perfect match for the breathtaking beauty.

"What's in the bag?" she asked as they wandered through the cooling evening air.

"A little surprise. Come on, I want to show you some-place special."

"Oh," she lifted her jade green eyes to his and smiled coyly.

Her stunning beauty always seemed to take him by surprise, leaving him dumfounded and void of all reason. Not that it should've. He had spent countless hours studying the angles and curves that made up his ever-love-lier mate.

Oliver had written music and lyrics in award-winning shows based solely on the color of her soulful eyes and the tempting way her top lip jutted out, only slightly larger than the lower. Peaches and cream wasn't just her scent, it was her coloring too. Glorious golden haired with pale skin that pinked up in various shades depending on what she was feeling.

When in the throes of passion, that blush travelled down her cheeks to her sweet, supple breast, all the way to her inner thighs. He licked his lips at the memory. She was in a word, superb.

And now he knew what he'd been missing the past two years. He understood why his work never seemed to satisfy him. Oliver had been missing his muse. He'd been missing Teresa.

"What?" she asked and he realized he'd stopped walking.

"Nothing. Well, not nothing. You're beautiful, you know," he stated.

"Ollie," she rolled her eyes, and he took lead.

Taking her hand he tugged her gently along and she followed him through the thicket of low standing trees. Just a few more feet, and he would be at his favorite spot in all of Indian Lake.

Way up high, a few dozen feet on the flat top of an enormous bolder that jutted out over the edge of the water was Oliver Pax's special place. He stood for a moment with her hand in his and just looked. This place was unique. It was close to his heart and he had never brought another living soul there before.

The air was crisp and cool as night softly fell all around them. The water glittered as tiny ripples made by fish and other animals stopping to drink broke the otherwise still waters. Those tiny breaks reflected the silvery moonlight. Like bits of broken silver, he thought.

It was breathtaking, beautiful, but it was nothing compared to her. Oliver removed the blanket from the rucksack and laid it across the hard stone. He took her hand and helped her to sit watching with interest as the long skirt slid up, revealing her long shapely legs.

She'd changed into a loose flowing dress that reached her ankles. It had short ruffles for sleeves the left her arms bare. Looking down he noted with approval a pair of flat sandals that slid easily off her dainty feet.

Tiny yellow flowers danced across the navy fabric of the dress. It draped across her splendid curves, molding to each dip and swell perfectly. It made his mouth water with wanting her, and his beast grunted in agreement.

"It's so quiet here. Still and perfect," Teresa murmured and laid her cheek across her knee as she watched the moon slowly climb higher in the near black skies.

Night fell quickly and Oliver had never felt so in tune with the elements as he did just then. Stars sparkled in the dark, velvety blanket that was the sky. They seemed to weave magic into the air as they looked down on Oliver and his mate from the heavens. He popped the cork on the bottle of Merlot he'd brought, and watched Teresa turn and gasp in delight.

"You brought wine?"

"Yes," he grinned at her surprise and he poured the dark red liquid into two metal tumblers.

He'd received a dozen of the polished gifts from Terrence to keep him and the rest of their circle of friends from constantly breaking glasses with their supernatural strength. As it was, they'd managed to dent only three of the set so far. He'd left those back at the cabin. He handed one unblemished cup to Teresa and his Bear growled lowly as their fingers brushed.

Mine. The animal inside of him longed to reconnect with her. Despite the fact they'd made love several times already, his beast wanted to re-claim his once lost beauty. For good this time.

Soon, he told his Bear.

"This is wonderful," she sighed, and sipped the fragrant liquid, "I love red wine."

"I remember," he slid behind her, opening his legs so that she could lean back against his chest.

"I used to only be able to buy the cheap stuff though," he shrugged.

"It was perfect then, and it is now," she said and he felt her heart beating rapidly right alongside his, "because of you, Oliver."

She set her cup down and turned in his arms. Kneeling between his legs, she reached up and pulled him to her. Oliver went without a fight. For her, he would do anything. Submit, give in, relinquish all control over his ordered life.

He would give her everything if he could just keep her. The best thing was, she asked for nothing except his love in return. That he would give her without hesitation.

"Need you, Ollie," she moaned into his mouth, and he readily allowed her entrance.

Her tongue twined with his, stirring up passion and long lost memories of nights spent entwined in his arms back in his tiny apartment in Brooklyn Heights. How he'd loved this woman!

Yes, he'd cursed her for leaving him, even as he'd yearned for her on those long lonely nights when he'd had no one to share the successes of his career, no one to simply hold in the coldness, to ward off the dark, and make his beast calm. But now, she was here, with him, and he and his Bear were positively elated to have her once more in his life.

Their kiss grew deeper and more urgent as Teresa tugged his sweatshirt over his head. He hissed as she raked her nails down his chest, kissing away the hurt with those maddening bee stung lips.

"Resa," he growled her name and changed position.

Laying her out on the blanket, he lifted her head and placed his sweatshirt beneath it as a makeshift pillow. Oliver leaned over her, inhaling her peaches and cream scent, swallowing it down as he soon would the very essence of that particular flavor from its sweetest core.

"Mine," he kissed her pretty mouth, undoing the buttons of her soft flowy dress one at a time.

He punctuated each tiny button's release with a thrust of his tongue, loving the way she submitted to his ministrations readily and with such unrehearsed enthusiasm. The night air cooled his sizzling skin as he shucked off every last article of clothing from his tall, muscular frame.

Oliver felt his Bear's power flickering just underneath

his human skin. The beast wanted to join in on the claiming, and he saw no reason to object. She belonged to all of him. Both he and his Bear held claim to both sides of her. It was the way of fated mates, he supposed.

"Need you," she writhed on the blanket, sighing as he parted the dress and helped her remove it from her arms.

She wore only a small pair of pink panties over her heavenly sex. They were darker just at the center, evidence of her need. His Bear rode him harder in that moment of realization. His gums ached and fingertips burned with the need to loosen claw and fang.

Not yet, he told his beast.

"Gonna give you everything you need, mate," he licked his lips.

He was actually drooling. Oliver Pax, renowned composer, and writer, was not only speechless in the face of such beauty as was his mate and lover, the mother of his cubs, lying naked in the moonlight, but he was motherfucking salivating as well.

She was all swells and valleys, dips and curves, acres of pale smooth skin for him to explore and cherish. He traced her pink tipped breasts with his fingers first, then his mouth, relishing her gasp as she arched off the floor and fitted herself more fully to him. She was fuller there now, rounded, and plump. So fucking beautiful, it made him want to curse and cry, growl, and roar, all at the same time.

"Yes, Ollie, oh yes," she praised as he slid down the slight swell of her soft belly to that scrap of pink that hid her treasures from him.

"Mine," he grunted the word and took the elastic band in his mouth looking up to capture her green gaze with his own.

"Yours," she echoed.

The sound of fabric tearing was loud in the quiet forest, but it only made them both that much more excited. He could practically feel her anticipation as if it was his own. Maybe it was.

Her Bear brushed against his mind and Oliver welcomed the Sow with open arms. She was his now. His to claim, his to love, and his to protect. Always.

Inhaling her heady musk, he parted her nether lips with his hands, gently brushing over the dark blonde curls that she thankfully kept natural, though neat he noted dutifully. She was gorgeous, sublime.

"Mine," he growled his new favorite word.

Oliver's eyes were glued to her face as he licked her with the flat of his tongue, parting her cheeks, he started at the top of her crevice down to her forbidden hole, all the way to that tiny, needy little bundle of nerves that held all her secrets and legions of untold pleasures.

Pleasures he intended to ring out until she had barely any breath left in her body. Yes. Tonight there was no holding back. Under the heavens he would worship her on this altar made of rock and earth, he would claim his mate and bind her to him for all time.

"Ollie!" she yelled, tugging on his hair, trying to pull him up, but he'd only just begun.

He used his strength to hold her carefully where he wanted her. Spread out before him, a sacrifice to his need. He continued to feast on his woman. Never before had he treated her to such thorough oral gratification, but this was the way of Shifter mates, and she was soon bucking her hips in time to his tongue's movements.

"Mate," he grunted, and added two digits to the mix, thrusting his fingers into her tight heat, and stretching her sex to better prepare her for him.

Tonight he was insatiable for her. He deserved to be, after all two years was a long time, and Oliver was a Shifter with a bear-sized appetite. He treated her to several more long swipes of his tongue before he settled on her clit.

His Bear surged forth and the rumbling growl added that little bit of extra to his ministration, causing his talented Bear's lips and tongue to vibrate against that needy little nub. Spreading her pussy lips, he worked his fingers in and out of her molten heat, all the while suckling that tiny nubbin.

Teresa yelled his name and arched her back. Good. He wanted her like that. Wild, desperate, and a little out of control.

Fuck, he grunted. He should've watched what he wished for as her claw tipped hands found his shoulders.

His beast growled with pleasure, taking her scratches as a sign she was marking him. Yes, why not? That was the way of creatures such as they. They scratched and bit, signs of love and ways of forging eternal bonds between couples. He wanted it all, and more. He doubled his efforts and soon she was crying out as her first orgasm swept through her.

Oliver held her through it, lapping at her pussy like the lovesick Bear he was until she could not even cry out. He looked up to find her eyes glowing beautifully with her Bear as she reached for him.

"My turn," she said and flipped them both in a move so strong and quick, he'd been completely unprepared for it.

His mind blanked and Oliver embraced the primitive thoughts of his Bear as he rose to meet her in a crashing embrace that made them both groan aloud. His cock grew even harder at the contact and she straddled him, lowering her slick heat down ever so slowly. Inch by inch she slid down his shaft until he was buried deep within her tight channel.

"Resa," he grunted her name.

A prayer, a chant, whatever have you, all he knew was he kept saying it as she began to move. Rocking her hips and taking him to paradise with every flex, ripple, and thrust.

"Ollie, mine, my mate," she mumbled and moved faster and harder, impaling herself over and over again on his cock.

He brought one hand up to cup her face and lower her to him, grunting with the effort it took to keep his passion in check. She felt so damn good, plunging into her silken depths was the ultimate for him, and fuck, he wanted to come so badly, but not yet.

Tension started deep in his gut as she milked his cock with her weeping pussy. Teresa's mouth opened in a silent scream as her moves became erratic. Yes, she was close and he knew just what to do to bring her over the edge.

"Mine," he growled the word and struck, re-marking his mate right on the scar from where he'd first laid claim to her.

"Oliver!" she yelled and her walls contracted with the force of her orgasm.

He sucked on her neck, swallowing her life's force, and solidifying the *matebond* that had grown so pale over the past couple of years apart. Snarling he released her flesh and pain exploded on his own left shoulder.

"Fuck," he grunted watching as she bit and claimed him with her own set of Shifter fangs.

His dick pulsed and cum filled her womb as pleasure unfurled and washed over him. The two of them clung to each other, trying to catch their breaths as ecstasy reigned supreme. It seemed to explode over the entire universe far as he was concerned. Never before had he ever felt such powerful joy and pleasure.

"Mine," she said and rocked her hips once more, and fuck him, if he didn't come even harder.

"Yours," he grunted, "mate."

After they'd packed up their makeshift picnic, Oliver helped Teresa back into her dress. She was a little wobbly on her feet, and he was the same, he grinned wickedly.

"What?" She asked.

"I was just thinking if we keep this up we'll both need walkers," he joked.

"Ha ha," she said and walked right up to him, twirling her arms around his neck brushing the already healing bite she'd given him delicately with her fingertips.

"This means you're mine now, right?"

"I've always been yours," he returned and kissed her quickly.

The entire world could change in the blink of an eye, but Oliver knew one thing to be true among all others. He would never stop wanting to kiss this woman.

The sound of multiple cars driving nearby had him turning around. He used his Bear's ears and nose to try and gain their scent and position.

"Strangers are nearing the cabin, let's get back."

Teresa's panicked expression met his and he understood real fear for the first time in his life. Thomas was back at the cabin.

"I'm going to shift," he explained and dropped the rucksack.

"I don't know if I can," she started.

"Don't worry. It's still new to you. Just climb on my back and I'll get us there quickly."

She did as he asked and together, they raced through

the woods. The sight that greeted him was as unwelcomed as it was unwanted.

Men in suits got out of two black SUVs. Two of them had long rifles in their hands. He discerned they were human with a whiff, but those goons weren't the ones he worried about. It was the sneering bastard who thought to come here himself.

"Teresa? Come out now, and I won't harm your *lover*," snarled Mathias Witherspoon.

Oliver growled low in his chest. Teresa slid off his back. He tried reaching her with his mind, wincing at his own shouted message.

No! Don't you dare. I got this.

She turned around and looked him in the eye, her posture exuded determination and he knew regardless of what he said, she would do as she needed. He saw that, respected it, understood it, and still, he feared for her safety.

"Let me talk to him, draw him away from the cabin and Thomas. If need be, you come in roaring."

"Teresa! You're only making it harder on yourself," Mathias' snide voice reached him easily.

It made his Bear want to rip the guy's head off, but he waited in the shadows of the trees, as his mate asked him to. He could scent her nervousness and fear, but even greater than those was her resolve.

"Hello, Mathias," she said startling all six men as she exited the woods and stood just to the side of his cabin.

"You do mean Father, don't you?" Mathias lied.

"No. I know you're not my father."

"Ah, well, good then we are past this charade. Come with me now. Bring your little animal bastard, and I won't expose Pax for the monster he is."

"I don't think so, Mathias, you see I finally understand that he is not the monster, neither am I for that matter."

"Is that so? Humans fornicating with animals. It's revolting," he spat the words at her and Oliver growled.

Teresa's head tilted towards him, a subtle sign that she was not ready for him to intervene yet. Except the men with guns were now trained on her. Oliver knew what to do.

"Your mother lied to me. I always wanted to marry her, but she was a filthy beast. And when I caught up with her it was too late, she wouldn't let me cure her. She'd already copulated with another and had you!"

"So you stole me from my mother?"

"Stole you? No, I saved you!"

"You're a bastard," she whispered as tears fell from her eyes.

"You are the bastard, and from the reports I got looks like the cycle has started again."

"My mother was a woman, a Shifter, and you killed her."

"Yes, she was an animal, and she wouldn't see reason. She didn't appreciate my cure for her ailment. Of course, I had to put her down."

"You are not curing anything," she screamed.

"So many doubters. I had to prove myself to others and now they see, you are proof my pills work!" he smiled evilly.

"No, you didn't cure me. You hurt me, kept me in a prison, lied to me, and look, *father*, I am still me," her anger was tangible.

She growled and snarled, embracing her Bear so quickly and savagely that Oliver couldn't help but feel pride in her quick transformation. She was learning to live with her Bear, but she was too far gone to see Mathias' signal to his men.

"That's too bad Teresa, I guess I will end you now, and experiment on your *cub*," he raised his hand and both men with the rifles took aim.

Teresa stood on her back legs and loosed a roar that shook the very earth while Oliver sped from the trees and with a mighty swipe of his paw took down both gunmen. After that, Teresa joined and together they subdued the rest of the men.

EPILOGUE

Teresa sat down on the couch with Thomas reading a storybook while Oliver cleared up the details of the clean-up with Jennifer.

Fortunately, no normals had happened upon the two enormous Grizzly Shifters protecting their cub and each other from Witherspoon Tech's president and his henchmen.

The two gunmen were lost causes, but Mathias Witherspoon and the others had survived with a few broken limbs and scratches.

They'd been taken away by whatever secret organization Jennifer worked for, and Teresa couldn't be sure, but she thought she saw a group of Draconian bi-peds land earlier.

She had asked Oliver if it was alright for her to stay in with Thomas since he'd been getting fussy and he'd readily agreed.

Good mate, her Bear chuffed.

Teresa agreed. She cuddled her son and finished the

story. After a few minutes, his breathing evened out and she realized he fell asleep.

"Love?" Ollie walked into the room with a smile and a couple of familiar faces.

"Hello again," Leandra said softly.

Teresa nodded and pursed her lips, she placed Thomas securely surrounded by pillows on the low settee and stood up.

"Hi, wow, you look better," Chance said and Oliver whacked him in the side, "What? Last time I saw her she was hooked up to a zillion machines," the half-Demon rubbed his arm and winked at her.

"Oh Chance," Leandra rolled her eyes.

"So, what the hell happened here? Why is the head of the Wyvern Protection Unit outside?" he whispered to Oliver who growled at him.

"Oh that," Teresa smiled, "long story. How about Oliver cooks us up some food, then we can discuss it?"

"Sounds good," Jennifer entered the room and nodded at the newcomers, "the guys have finished cleaning up outside and I am famished."

"Okay," Oliver cocked his head at her and raised an eyebrow, "if my mate can help me for a minute in the kitchen?"

She nodded and followed him down the hall while the other adults took seats in the dining room promising to keep an eye out for little Thomas.

"Are you alright?" he asked and gathered her close to him.

"I have never been better. I know who I am and where I belong for the first time in my life," she said simply.

"I love you, Teresa, I almost died when I saw those guns

trained on you," he whispered and dropped his head to kiss her.

"I wasn't scared because you were there. I knew my Grizzly Bear mate would never let anything bad happen to me," she smiled against his mouth feeling the pride her words encouraged to soar through him.

"Mine," he said.

"Yeah, yeah, she's yours, whatever, but when am I gonna see my pages, Pax?" interrupted Chance from the doorway.

Teresa's eyes shot to the half-Demon and her Sow rose up to greet him with a snarl. She did not like being interrupted while she was with her mate.

"Okay, we can discuss it later, no biggie," the smart man shrugged and backed out of the kitchen.

Teresa heard the thwack of his mate's slap and smiled. She had to remember to thank Leandra later.

"Now. where were we?" she asked and kissed her mate hard on the lips.

"There is good," Oliver grunted.

"I am yours," she echoed his earlier statement, "but you're mine too," she pulled him down for a harder, longer kiss.

The strength of their *matebond* pulsed through her and Teresa felt closer than ever to Oliver. Everything seemed to multiply in intensity now that she'd embraced her inner beast.

Oh yes, she thought, she was going to like being a Bear.

"After all this time, I have a Grizzly lover of my own, sweet mate," Oliver stole her breath with another meeting of lips, this one the sweetest kiss of them all.

"Wait till later," he winked, "we'll compose symphonies

together in the dark," he promised and she bit her lips to keep from groaning.

Side by side, the couple set about preparing food for their family and their guests and Teresa's heart swelled with love.

Tomorrow looked brighter already, she thought as she took in the brilliant sun blinking overhead. Now that her family was together all the tomorrows were going to be stunning.

THE END

BEFORE YOU GO

STOP! *Before you go, sign up for my newsletter and get the latest on my releases, giveaways, freebies and more:*

SUBSCRIBE HERE

ABOUT THE AUTHOR

Hello!

I'm C.D. Gorri, Bestselling Steamy Paranormal Romance, Urban Fantasy YA Bestselling Author, and Creator of the Grazi Kelly Universe.

I've always been an avid reader, and I have a profound love for books and literature. When I'm not writing or taking care of my family I can usually be found with a book or tablet in my hand. I live in my home state of New Jersey with my husband, our children, and our dogs, Dash and Chewie.

I'm a busy mom of three and finding time for leisurely reading is never easy, so I write stories that are fast-paced, yet detailed with satisfying conclusions. If I thought making time to read was difficult, I was in for a huge surprise when I started writing! But now that I started, I can't picture myself doing anything else! I love writing powerful women and strong heroes who face relatable problems in supernatural settings! I plan on increasing the Grazi Kelly Universe with each and every story I publish. You can follow me on social media to keep up to date on all my new releases and events!

Looking for steamy Paranormal Romance, well I have

several series available and am adding more all the time. I love helping sassy, curvy heroines and sexy heroes find their HEAs in my books! I write about Werewolves, Bear Shifters, Dragons, Tigers, Witches, Romani, Lynxes, Foxes and more in my PNR! Fated mates who find each other and always get their happily ever afters.

Want to know how it all began? Enter the Grazi Kelly Universe with Wolf Moon: A Grazi Kelly Novel #1, my very first YA/Urban Fantasy book that sets the stage for the universe I write in. You can also start my PNR with the Macconwood Pack. Pick up Charley's Christmas Wolf today!

Thank you for dropping by and happy reading!

del mare alla stella,
    C.D. Gorri
    *Bestselling Author

P.S.

You can follow me on Twitter @cgor22, Instagram CDGorri, Google+, tumblr, Pinterest, Goodreads, and Facebook http://www.facebook.com/cdgorribooks or visit my website www.cdgorri.com.

*I am proud to be a two-time Smashwords USA Today Happy Ever After Hot List Indie Author, #1 iBooks PNR, #1 Amazon New Releases, and Barnes & Noble Bestseller!

*Before you go any further, sign up for my newsletter and get the latest on my releases, giveaways, freebies and more:

https://www.subscribepage.com/cdgorri

facebook.com/cdgorribooks
twitter.com/cgor22
instagram.com/cdgorri
bookbub.com/authors/c-d-gorri

Hello!

Thank you so much for reading my book!

The Grazi Kelly Universe is growing by leaps and bounds and I have plans to increase it even further! Be sure to check out how the Macconwood Pack all started with *Wolf Bride* and *Charley's Christmas Wolf.*

I've got Werewolves, Dhampirs, Dragons, Thunderbirds, Tigers, Vampires, Witches and more! You can find my books in Purely Paranormal Pleasures, MTWorlds, Evel Worlds, and more to come.

If you enjoy steamy paranormal romance with curvy heroines and sexy heroes, you've come to the right place! Check my website for upcoming features here: https:/www.cdgorri.com.

It's back to my writing cave for now!

del mare alla stella,

C.D. Gorri

CONNECT WITH C.D. GORRI

Follow me here:
https://www.facebook.com/Cdgorribooks
https://twitter.com/cgor22
https://www.bookbub.com/profile/c-d-gorri

Visit my website to find out more about my supernatural world also known as the Grazi Kelly Universe!
https://www.cdgorri.com

***Sign up for my newsletter and get the latest on my releases, giveaways, freebies and more:**
https://www.subscribepage.com/cdgorri

OTHER TITLES BY C.D. GORRI

Young Adult Books:

Wolf Moon: A Grazi Kelly Novel Book 1

Hunter Moon: A Grazi Kelly Novel Book 2

Rebel Moon: A Grazi Kelly Novel Book 3

Winter Moon: A Grazi Kelly Novel Book 4

Chasing The Moon: A Grazi Kelly Short 5

Blood Moon: A Grazi Kelly Novel 6

*Get all 6 books NOW AVAILABLE IN A BOXED SET:

The Complete Grazi Kelly Novel Series

Casting Magic: The Angela Tanner Files 1

Keeping Magic: The Angela Tanner Files 2

Paranormal Romance Books:

Macconwood Pack Novel Series:

Charley's Christmas Wolf: A Macconwood Pack Novel 1

Cat's Howl: A Macconwood Pack Novel 2

Code Wolf: A Macconwood Pack Novel 3

The Witch and The Werewolf: A Macconwood Pack Novel 4

To Claim a Wolf: A Macconwood Pack Novel 5

Macconwood Pack Tales Series:

Wolf Bride: The Story of Ailis and Eoghan A Macconwood Pack Tale 1

Summer Bite: A Macconwood Pack Tale 2

His Winter Mate: A Macconwood Pack Tale 3

Snow Angel: A Macconwood Pack Tale 4

Charley's Baby Surprise: A Macconwood Pack Tale 5

Home for the Howlidays: A Macconwood Pack Tale 6

A Silver Wedding: A Macconwood Pack Tale 7

Mine Furever: A Macconwood Pack Tale 8 (as seen in Hearts & Bite Marks Anthology)

Macconwood Pack Tales BOXED SETS:

The Macconwood Pack Tales Volume 1

Shifters Furever: The Macconwood Pack Tales Volume 2

The Falk Clan Tales:

The Dragon's Valentine: A Falk Clan Novel 1

The Dragon's Christmas Gift: A Falk Clan Novel 2

The Dragon's Heart: A Falk Clan Novel 3

The Dragon's Secret: A Falk Clan Novel 4

Dragon Mates: The Falk Clan Complete Series Boxed Set

The Bear Claw Tales:

Bearly Breathing: A Bear Claw Tale 1

Bearly There: A Bear Claw Tale 2

Bearly Tamed: A Bear Claw Tale 3

Bearly Mated: A Bear Claw Tale 4

*The Complete Bear Claw Tales (Books 1-4)

The Barvale Clan Tales:

Polar Opposites: The Barvale Clan Tales 1

Polar Outbreak: The Barvale Clan Tales 2

Purely Paranormal Pleasures:

Marked by the Devil: Purely Paranormal Pleasures

Mated to the Dragon King: Purely Paranormal Pleasures

Claimed by the Demon: Purely Paranormal Pleasures

Christmas with a Devil, a Dragon King, & a Demon: Purely Paranormal Pleasures (short story)

Vampire Lover: Purely Paranormal Pleasures

Zodiac Shifters:

Bound by Air: The Wardens of Terra Book 1: A Zodiac Shifters Book

Star Kissed: A Wardens of Terra Short

Waterlocked: The Wardens of Terra Book 2: A Zodiac Shifters Book

Moon Kissed: A Wardens of Terra Short

The Maverick Pride Tales:

Purrfectly Mated: Paranormal Dating Agency: A Maverick Pride Tale 1

Purrfectly Kissed: Paranormal Dating Agency: A Maverick Pride Tale 2

Purrfectly Trapped: Paranormal Dating Agency: A Maverick Pride Tale 3

Dire Wolf Mates:

Shake That Sass: Sassy Ever After: Dire Wolf Mates Book 1

Breaking Sass: Sassy Ever After: Dire Wolf Mates 2

Dark Moon Falls II:

Foster (as seen in Dark Moon Falls II anthology)

Stand Alones:

The Enforcer

Coming Soon:

Grizzly Lover: Purely Paranormal Pleasures

Chinchilla and the Devil: A FUCN'A Book

Mine Furever (extended release)

Conall's Mate: A Macconwood Pack Novel 6

Purrfectly Caught: Paranormal Dating Agency: A Maverick Pride Tale 4

Purrfectly Timed: Paranormal Dating Agency: A Maverick Pride Tale 5

Pinch of Sass: Sassy Ever After: Dire Wolf Mates 3

Hold the Sass: Sassy Ever After: Dire Wolf Mates 4

MORE FROM MY FELLOW PURELY
PARANORMAL PLEASURES
AUTHORS...

Manifestations

The Cure

Uncharted

Coming Soon

The Pride Within

The Chronic Collection Series

(Contemporary Romance Stand Alone Collection)

Down by the Willow Tree

To Hell With Carpets

Coming Soon a New Series Spinoff of The Chronic Collection!

Just Breathe

Just Be

Just Believe

Poetry

The Fast Still Life

The Puzzle Called Life

Blue Water Baptism

Group Anthologies

Tempt Me: A Romance Limited Edition Collection

(*Coming Soon from EveL Worlds*)

The Turtle and the Hare

For More Information Please Visit: https://www.bookbub.com/profile/amanda-kimberley

Full Moon Series

World of Azglen: The Full Moon of Charley Rabbit with M. Mattern and J.C. Estall

Congregation of Darkness with J.C. Estall

Full Moon Falling Faster with M. Mattern

A Quanta of Magic with M. Mattern

Roue of the Dragon With M. Mattern

Dragon Fire Halls of Ash and Marble with M. Mattern

Blue Moon with L. Gauthier

Vampire Princess Trilogy

The Vampire Princess

The Vampire Queen

Vampire Empress

Purely Paranormal Pleasures

Sex With a Selkie

Sex With a Selkie 2

Goldilocks and Her Harem of Bears

Menopausal Magic

(Coming Soon)

Menopausal Magic 2: Thandie's Wedding

Stand Alone PNR/Horror

Teasing My Inner Vampire

In the Penumbra of the Gods: The Pandora Sanction

Damned by Desire

Three and a Half Wishes

The Handsome Devils Modeling Club

My Own Personal Vampire

Sex Slave to My Vampire Billionaire Step Brothers (A Reverse Harem Tale)

Cinderelavant: A Reverse Harem Fairytale Retelling

It Came: A Cozy Christmas Horror Story

Vampire Orphanage

Shock of Night

Blood So Pure

Miss Me

The Sandbox

The Halloween Girls

The Ghost Pepper Sagas

Three and a Half Wishes

Mistletoe and Fangs

Sex With Zombies

Beat You Down

The Girl in the Sand

Dreams to Bear

The Semen Flower (Alien Lullabies)

Dark Secrets Of A Dhampir

Shock Of Night

Blood So Pure: A Jack Silver Adventure

Zombiewalk

Hot Rocket Ride

Science Fiction

Riveted

Cold Word

Co-Written PNR/Horror/YA

Crimson with KC Harper

I'll Make You Scream with L. Gauthier

Over My Grave with L. Ashby

Pearl and Ruby with Sheri Williams

Hour of the Witch Spinners with Scarlet Darkwood

The Forest of the Bleeding Trees with M. Mattern

Strident House with M. Mattern

The Third Flame with SJ Davis

Andy of the Damned with Marcus Mattern

Anthologies

The Horror Collection: Purple Edition: THC Book 3

Damsels of Distress (Strong Heroine Series Book 1)

Beautiful Nightmare: A Women in Horror Anthology

Another Beautiful Nightmare: A Women in Horror Anthology

Demons, Devils and Denizens of Hell

Demons, Devils and Denizens of Hell Book 2

Vindicta (The Liquidator Wars Book 1)

A Book to Last the Year: Volume 3—Horror/Dark/Very Dark (A Calendar Anthology)

A Paranormal Solstice Anthology

Painted Mayhem

To Learn More About P. Mattern please visit: https://www.
bookbub.com/profile/p-mattern

P.S.

Don't forget to tell me how you liked this story by leaving your honest review! *No pressure.* 😉

A review can be one or two short sentences where you simply state whether you enjoyed the story and would recommend it to someone! It is a huge help to authors and the best way for us to reach larger audiences so that we can keep writing the stories you love!

Thank you so much!

Xoxo!

Del mare alla stella,

C.D. Gorri

Excerpt from Marked By The Devil:

PROLOGUE

Snap! Flash! Snap! Bang!

"Over here! The Dark Prince is by the window!"

Click! Bang! Snap!

"Oh, for fuck's sake," Avail growled. He could feel that secret part of him pushing to be released. Power pulsed through his veins, his beast demanding to be set free, but he fought the temptation.

Snap! Flash! The horde of paparazzi swarmed outside the entrance to the Leeds Foundation, snapping pictures and banging on the polished reinforced glass doors in hopes of catching a glimpse of him. *Their prey.*

If they only knew. He growled aloud, eyes flashing at the throng below. The man they hunted was not the useless, spoiled playboy they took him for. Avail Leeds was something more. A predator. Not like those uncouth vultures circling with their cameras and cheap shots.

He was the real thing. A creature humankind built into legend with stories of midnight encounters. He snorted a harsh laugh. *If only I could show them. Grrrr.*

They'd been there since daybreak hoping to get a statement or a picture of him, but Avail had managed to dodge them. He was no stranger to this kind of game. *Unfortunately for him. Sigh.* They'd dubbed him the "Naughty Dark Prince" years ago, recording his exploits and reporting them with more than a touch of exaggeration, as a constant source of entertainment for *normals* the world over.

As heir to the Leeds fortune, Avail had been in the spotlight since birth. Especially after his parent's tragic death when he was an infant. His grandparents had brought him up with the finest education and surroundings a boy could have. So, yes, he was known to indulge in a bit of luxury and sport in between his family's foundation and other philanthropic works.

The Leeds family was enormously wealthy. The money had come to the family at first from the land itself. Natural resources like coal and oil had started the family's legacy. Later on, they'd dabbled in manufacturing, then real estate and development. Now the family was known for their charity.

Avail himself had increased their holdings by playing the stock market and investing in several internet start-ups. He certainly had a marvelous head for figures. The mathematical and the female kind.

He gritted his teeth at the reminder. The latter had, once again, caused him this current headache. Women would surely be the death of him, or so his grandmother promised. Often. *Oh dear. Grandmother is certain to be angry this time.*

"Denise!" Avail groaned his secretary's name as he looked out his office window.

So many of them are here this time. Ugh. He slumped back in his Perigold executive chair. The exotic French walnut was highly polished and smelled of lemons. The seat was made from the leather of a sixteen-point stag that his great-grandfather had taken down himself. He remembered that day.

Hunting with Grandfather was often the best time of his life. After all, he'd taught Avail everything he knew about controlling his inner demons, so to speak. He sure missed the old man.

His darling grandmother ordered the leather made from the buck's skin to be turned into this bit of posh office furniture for Avail when he took over as president of the Leeds Foundation. Conditioned with only the best mixtures of Mink and Neatsfoot oils, the chair was fucking amazing, if he did say so himself. Soft and strong, perfect for his six-foot four-inch, two-hundred and forty-pound frame.

He was certainly grateful for it as he slunk down into the buttery depths and cradled his head in his hands. It was only seven o'clock in the morning. How did those vultures find him so quickly?

"What have you done now?" *Why does her voice have to reach that pitch?* He cringed.

"Just the usual, Denise," he answered with a grin.

His silk shirt of the night before hung open revealing a large expanse of his muscled chest, evenly covered in a dusting of black hair. It matched the midnight dark strands atop his head that earned him the hated moniker *"Naughty Dark Prince"*.

Of course, if he'd bothered to stay out of the public eye the name would probably be forgotten. *Fat chance.* Avail couldn't help himself. He simply loved life, women, and parties. Usually, in that order.

He didn't bother to button his shirt or his pants as Denise stomped across the floor in those ridiculous heels she wore. The older woman had seen him in far worse shape. He could use a shower and shave, ooh, and some breakfast.

A bloody steak and half a dozen eggs should do it, but even as he thought it his stomach revolted. *Ugh. See what happens when we mix whiskey and magic!* His Devil growled inside of him and Avail groaned aloud. The magic had been a bit much, but the little Witch deserved it. Taunting him for not being interested in her obvious wiles.

The glare coming from Denise had him refocusing his attention on the motherly woman. *Ouch.* She could singe toast with that look! *So loving*, he thought. His secretary of seven years cared about him. That was nice.

"Well, Denise, I suppose you want to know what happened-"

"Oh, a night of wining and dining the little trust fund baby? What's to know? Did *little pookie* not like getting kicked out of bed at 3AM?"

Denise Reynolds stood over Avail with a large, steaming mug of his favorite French roast, served black, in one hand. In the other was a large cup of tomato juice and six aspirin. Otherwise he might have growled at her insolence. *As if.* He loved the crotchety older woman.

Her white hair was sprayed straight up like spindles guarding a castle. The sight was a bit harsh on his poor bloodshot eyes. *Yes*, he'd had far too good a time last night, but it wasn't with *little pookie* as much as it was with the whiskey he'd imbibed. *And the magic he'd wielded.*

It was nearing the last quarter moon and Avail's beastie had been up for some good old-fashioned debauchery. As was the little Witch he'd brought along for the ride. Bambi was a trust fund baby and a Witch. He'd met her at *The Thirsty Dog* where he'd gone to partake in some booze and dancing, perhaps a little nookie with a stranger.

He thought he'd found the perfect partner for the evening in the wicked Bambi. The woman had been down for just about anything. Including skinny dipping in the frigid Blue Hole which was just a few miles from his home.

He'd used a few tricks with some ancient runes and conjured a little light show while they swam. He'd even allowed his Devil to play a little bit as well. Hoping for a little suck and blow afterwards. *Not the card game.*

And then it had all gone wrong. Bambi had wanted promises with her sex. That was a serious no in his book. Then the taunting came and out she went. *Like a light.*

"Well?"

"Oh Denise, what can I say? She wanted more than an evening's entertainment. I simply didn't see us headed that way."

"Well, normally I'd say the girl had standards, but uh, I don't think so."

He stretched as he swallowed his aspirin and downed the tomato juice. Avail held his hot coffee carefully. Denise had a sadistic side and he'd caught her trying to burn his Devil once or twice over the years.

"Humph. How is *that* too hot for you?" She rolled her eyes and gathered the empty glass as he continued to wait for his coffee to cool down.

"I told you before, I'm not that kind of Devil, Denise," he murmured and sipped the brew as it reached the perfect temperature. *Heaven.* He continued to sip with his eyes closed ignoring everything but the smooth warm liquid as it slid down his throat.

"Really, Avail? You took *that* silicone doll to the Blue Hole! Your grandmother is going to be furious with you."

"Yes, yes, I know. Wait, how did you know?" He frowned.

The swimming spot had been shunned by locals for decades, but the Leeds family still enjoyed the crystal-clear waters. They were fed by an underground glacier though some still claim to be baffled by its existence. *Whatever.*

Still, he knew better than to take a normal to one of his family's private haunts. He also knew better than to use magic in front of anyone. But he'd figured it was alright since Bambi was in fact a Witch. Even better, she had her own money. So he didn't need to worry about her motives. Ideally, she'd been looking for a little light fun on a Friday night. That was all! *How wrong he'd been.*

"Avail, you need to see this."

"Hmm? What?" He turned and looked at the older woman who was staring at the television with her mouth hanging open.

"Pookie took pictures! *Ha!* Looks like you've finally did it this time. And look, an interview too-"

"Oh fuck! Turn it up!"

"Leedsy is a very naughty boy! Mmm hmm. He fed me whiskey and oysters on a silk sheet by the pool...I tell you the truth I didn't mind spanking him, but the ball and gag was where I drew the line. I like it when my men talk dirty, you know?...Of course, that's true!...Well, he insisted on wearing my thong as a choker...Yes, I'd be willing to go out with him again. He is a big boy after all, and his endurance is divine... I found his size to be more than adequate though his oral skills were slightly exaggerated...but that is nothing compared to what happened afterwards...yeah we both saw him...the actual Jersey Devil..."

For fucks sake! On and on, the insipid woman spewed lie after lie for the next twenty minutes while displaying scenes of Avail swimming while imbibing of the locally distilled artisan whiskey, *Devil's Bite,* straight from the bottle.

How he loved that fiery smooth alcohol! Mason Lane, his friend and the owner of the distillery, created the label specially for Avail.

The perfect blend of *piri,* or African devil peppers, and burnt sugar, *Devil's Bite* is distilled and aged for five years in casks created from local oak trees.

Avail had cases of the stuff back at Leeds Mansion. His childhood and now permanent home, as his grandmother was determined to globetrot for the rest of her days. Especially since grandfather was dead and buried.

He hoped this story wouldn't carry to Egypt, where his grandmother was currently spending her time. She deserved. The shrill ring of the telephone snapped him out of his musings.

"Avail here."

"Mr. Leeds, this is Mr. Henries, your grandmother demanded I find you."

"Hello, Henries. Well, I'm at work. so I guess you found me."

"Yes. I figured as much, and I don't need to remind you that the launch of our newest campaign for Leeds Foundation, *the one you initiated,* to raise funds for at risk youth, begins *today*."

"You don't need to remind me. Our campaign, *Leeds Foundation, Believe in the Future,* was *my idea* as you said, Henries."

"Yes, well, Mrs. Leeds was not a fan of this campaign. Coupled with your latest *adventures,* I am tasked to advise you that your grandmother is seriously displeased. She suggests you go home, Avail."

"What? But there is a lot to do-"

"Denise will handle it. You are to go back to Leeds Mansion and *'wait out the storm'*. Those are her exact words"

"Tell my grandmother that she knows what happens at the end of the week-"

"She is aware." Avail could practically see the blank expression on the lawyer's face through the phone. He'd never quite pinpointed what sort of supernatural the man was, but his loyalty and devotion to the Leeds family had spanned decades, *twelve or so to be exact.*

"It's almost the last quarter moon, Henries, and I have no intention of staying-"

"*Mr. Leeds*," his voice deepened, "your grandmother has told me that if you refuse, she shall be forced to defer back to your grandfather's original will. The one where you do not inherit until you have achieved thirty-eight years unless you marry before then. Do you recall the terms?"

"Yes," Avail growled into the receiver, "I recall the terms. Tell Grandmother, not to worry. I am on my way home."

CHAPTER ONE

"No, no, no," Stephanie slammed her hands down on the steering wheel of her tiny car. The tiny Smart car was cute as pie to look at. Totally worth it too. Well, when she'd lived in the city it had been worth it.

But out in the boonies, also known as the beach town of Maccon City, New Jersey, the damn automobile was more trouble than it was worth.

The thing could hardly make it up the sandy dirt covered private road that would soon lead to the beautifully preserved cobblestone driveway of the illustrious Leeds family.

According to her research, the Leeds were one of the original founding families of the Pine Barrens of New Jersey. Like her own family tree, theirs dated all the way back to revolutionary times. *What an interesting coincidence!*

Not that she knew all that much about the state or her ancestors having grown up in western Pennsylvania. Stephanie had recently moved to Maccon City to be closer to her new job. A job she landed with the help of her two BFF's.

She missed Cora and Leandra every day. The three of them did everything together! Had since they were teens at the exclusive, another word for stuck-up, *Mrs. Parker's School for Girls*. Tucked away from normal teenagers in the wilds of Pennsylvania, the three of them had formed a little sisterhood. Vowing to always be there for each other.

They attended college together at the Brandywine campus of Penn State, opting to rent an apartment over dorm life. They even stayed, continuing to live together, after graduation. All working jobs in nearby Philadelphia.

Everything was fine until Cora got a job at a bank overseas. Stephanie was happy for her brilliant mathematician friend. *You bet she was.* Only, her heart squeezed at seeing her go.

That shocking announcement was soon followed by another from Leandra. Her other roommate having decided to move to New York City to pursue her dreams of becoming a stage performer.

Another devastating blow to the rather introverted Stephanie. Her feelings of abandonment aside, she managed to be happy for them both. Besides, they had helped her find the perfect job and town to move to before they left. *In true BFF fashion.*

I miss those two, she thought as she curved around the long, winding road. Too much time had passed between visits. Sure, they still sent her emails and texts. *Especially Cora.*

Stephanie was almost overwhelmed by her constant barrage of the latest dating apps and trends for her perpetually single friend. *Sigh.* They knew her too well. *Fact check:*

She was way too shy to go to bars or clubs without her two BFFs there to bolster her.